AND...
THE CROSSROAD

AND...
THE CROSSROAD

BIPIN BARAL

PARTRIDGE
A Penguin Random House Company

To order additional copies of this book, contact
Partridge India
000 800 10062 62
orders.india@partridgepublishing.com

www.partridgepublishing.com/india

Acknowledgements

This venture is something that has always remained as part of my dreams and it would remain so if I was not blessed with the help, encouragement and support of the following people.

First and foremost I would like to express my gratitude and sincere thanks to Nirmika Subba, Deependra Sharma, Marvin Lepcha and Bedika Rai not only for helping me with the editing but also for their valuable suggestions and feedbacks.

I am privileged to have met Vivek Mishra in my life. I thank him for his edits and insights. His unflinching support right through has certainly been instrumental in shaping my dream.

I also want to thank Rasik Chettri from the bottom of my heart for his relentless support and being there for me in times of need.

I have amazing group of friends who have always encouraged and supported me in my endeavors. I want to thank all you guys especially Prakash, Wangdi, Layden, Mingma, Millen, Aanchal, Mahendra, Maan, Reetesh, Aakansha, Sudhan,

Sashil, Bristrit, Deechen, Siddhant, Lhendup, Rajiv, Aman, Ashish, Pemba, Sonam, Sagar, Manan, Amit and Kiran.

I am thankful to Sikkim University and its cafeteria for I have used their premises to write this story. I especially want to thank the cafeteria boys—Prakash, Simon, Roshan, Bishal, Passang, Nagen, Pradeep, Tilak, Binod, Bijay and others for their support.

I also want to thank my friends, brothers and sisters in the University for their encouragement and support.

I thank all my relatives for their constant inspiration.

I would like to thank my parents, the Gods I can see, hear and embrace at all times. Thank you for being with me through thick and thin.

I also want to thank all those people who have helped me in one way or the other and whose names I may have failed to mention. Your part is sincerely appreciated.

Last but not the least I thank God almighty for this life, this work.

Thank you all with all my heart.

In memory of my Hachiko
(11th June 2010 - 7th February 2015)
Without you my home will always be incomplete!

I believe there's a reason,
For every change of season
We meet to depart and depart to meet
And in all meeting and departing session
Some leave us with imprinting impression
I am fortunate to have met good ones
Especially the one I dearly miss
I have realized that it takes profound emotions to write
And in my case it was pain
Don't know how well I have lived up to it
But it's none like being able to ventilate one's emotions
So for you, to write a story I take the pen
And travel far and deep into my eternal memory lane.

Prologue

This man I intend to recount to you about has nothing out of the ordinary. He is very much around the commons and you won't have to go too far to find him. He is in fact so ordinary that I want to baptize him not as another Tom, or Dick but Harry, and in this case I chose Hari. He is Hari, son of Rudra Hari and grandson of saint Narhari, the epitomized freedom fighter from the hills. Hills here refer to the terrain in India famous for tea, timber and tourism—Darjeeling, the Queen of Hills. This also means that I don't have a hero per say for this story since he does not have any heroic credibility, neither does he have a rogue persona nor is he a desperado. So I just have a protagonist; protagonist mainly because the story is about his life, romance and expectations.

This is a tale of an imperfect dude in search of perfection; a perfection in love, to be loved and to love.

He is a simple, honest and an innocuous soul, rare enough to be found everywhere, every time. Hari, man of few words whose imperfections speak volumes and it is these imperfections that I want to depict and capture in my writing. His imperfections are so gracious that his virtues become inspiring and his nature enthuses my tired yet vindictive soul to write about him. His imperfections make him dreary, drab and dull yet the same imperfections make him insanely sweet and absurdly beautiful or absurdly sweet and insanely beautiful.

Everyone falls in love and everyone has a love story. Some love stories are so blessed that from its inception, it's as perfect as pure gold. It has that catching shine, a glow that captivates one's imagination. It has weight and it has value and with each passing moment the value increases. Such love stories cannot be ignored and they do not go unnoticed. Those are like the stars that twinkle every night, always there yet so hard to reach. Then, there are some that take a different turn. It takes us to a world filled with heartaches, despair and loneliness, literally paralyzing our sane lives and turning them into something chaotic and anarchic; a place that is suffocating, gloomy and frantic. But still, in those dark corners, love remains exactly and precisely the same as it is in those blessed love stories, because love is the very light that shines equally on all facades, be it smooth or rough, dry or wet.

Hari is my friend and I dare write about him and claim to be so familiarly accustomed with him only because I have spent years with him and know him like two peas in the same pod. I don't claim that the dialogues written are verbatim accounts of conversations but yes their essences are alive and intact. I have been careful not to lose the audacity of honesty during the translation of the impressions into writing. If I were to measure this novel in mathematical terms, I would compute this at the ratio of 70:30, meaning, I have imprinted facts in the major chunk of the book and have given way for fiction in the remaining portion.

In crux, this story is an amalgamation of imperfections v/s perfections in the realm of every romantic strife.

Love stories are shaped, sustained and smudged
only for the sake of loving it more

Part I

Chapter I

The Maverick

Hari had a mundane childhood and a mediocre teenage life with nothing exciting to share about. He was average in studies and would always remain a 'Backyard Chicken' in life just refusing to come to the centre stage. He was neither famous nor notorious; an innocuous soul who hardly did anything exceptional to get noticed. He was a testimony of what Derozio calls 'An Unknown Citizen', 'A' someone whom nobody would care to remember or recognize. He studied in a co-educational institution but could never be comfortable in the company of girls. His timidity forbade him to mingle around with others and his shy blushes made him a near introvert. He neither bunked his classes nor was he ever involved in crazy streaks. A benevolent son of an ethical father and the righteous grandson of a patriotic freedom fighter, Hari always had to abide by the code of morality proudly cherished by the family lineage. Never was he thrown out of his classes, nor did he ever trouble his parents or anybody else. Hari was an epitome of Gandhian perfection so fondly cherished by his grandfather that he could never imagine to see anything that was wrong or hear anything which was bad or speak anything foul.

Poor Hari! He was but a man trapped in his own oddities.

I don't remember when I saw him first but I do know that he was the first to talk to me many years back when I was in the initial years of my college days. My family had newly shifted to another village in a fairly remote area and had started building a very badly architected house which had to be renovated shortly incurring a considerable loss of money. Till the completion of the new house, I was living with my family at my grandpa's house which happened to be few 'turns' ahead of Hari's home—the great Indian freedom fighter's bungalow.

Geographical locations in the hills are generally determined by the number of turnings the places are located on along the serpentine roads. The roads turn in and out and they function as the prime locater and interestingly act as proper nouns for proper addresses. So my house is three turnings ahead of my grandpa's house which is at a distance of five turnings from Hari's house. Consequently, my grandpa's house falls at 6th mile, mine at 5th and Hari's at 7th mile!

I had come home to Kalimpong for a self proclaimed vacation from my college for three weeks. Thanks to my contacts with the general secretary of the student union, the 75 percentage attendance though mandatory was still not mandatory.

Kalimpong, one of the sub divisions of Darjeeling is known for its temperate climate, educational institutions and orchids. Situated at an altitude of 1250 meters with sound geographical establishment, it offers a rich variety of flora. The small town, in its entire splendor has therefore remained a pristine destination for tourists. In the past it also used to be a gateway between Tibet and India and is still strategically located.

*

It was one of the evenings during this particular vacation that I happened to meet Hari. I had gone to 5th mile, the location of my new house, to see the construction in progress. I was sitting at the verandah watching the passersby. I saw him.

He was young, probably a couple of years younger to me, lean man of short stature and in school uniform carrying a leather satchel but not looking smart at all. He wore a grey trouser which was either out of fashion or badly tailored. I guess it was a combination of both. A grey sweater, probably a size bigger and a white shirt made the look barely okay in the end. He had a small face, a bit long nose and bore a tanned look. His lips were stretched across his face, seemingly in a permanent smile! Above his lips was a faint collage of moustache which could be counted if anybody was interested. His hair was neatly combed and was parted on the side. It seemed like a river flowing from one end to the other and the conspicuous greasiness gave me an impression that the hair oil he used must have been pure mustard oil. He had clear, black, but unattractive eyes. He seemed calm and relaxed as if nothing in this world bothered him, not even the black fly that was hovering around his head for quite some time.

"Hello," He screamed from nowhere. I greeted him back, he continued.

"Is this your house?"

I replied infirmly.

"I have been seeing you for some time now so just enquired, hope you don't mind."

I didn't know what to say so just nodded to suggest that I didn't.

"Which school you study?" He asked.

"I study in a college in Siliguri," I said with much gusto.

"Oh!" He said, "I am in 12th standard at Kumudini Homes."

After a brief conversation he went his way and I took mine. He quickly lapsed into oblivion from my memory.

*

Probably a week had passed by when we met again in the market. I was busy buying some household commodities when I felt a tap on my shoulder. I turned to look around, it was Hari.

"Hello, how are you doing?" He asked.

"I am fine and you?" I said.

"I am fine too," He replied and went on, "I don't see you these days, where are you?"

"I was out of station," I replied to make my reply succinct.

"Are you free?" He asked and I don't know why I said yes, though I was not. Probably that's fate; when fate wants us to meet, it creates situations though it is also true that sometimes we create it. Whatever be the reason, we were now seated face to face in a small restaurant. I discerned that he never was of my genre and his views on certain aspects and especially his talks bored me to death. We both had different credos; we were poles apart. He had rather a dowdy outlook. I had had enough of his boring talks but couldn't ask him to stop. The restaurant seemed to me like a desert with his talks—a sheer monologue.

I chose to have a bottle of beer to evade my boredom and to change the topic. I ordered the waiter for a bottle of local beer 'Hit'. For a snack I opted for a locally improvised delicacy consisting of Wai-Wai (instant noodle) mixed with *Dallae* (local chili), raw mustard oil and finely chopped onions. As I placed the order and turned towards him, his gestures somehow suggested that I had committed a heinous crime by ordering myself a drink.

"You drink beer too?" He inquired, raising his eyebrows. Probably he was already startled with my fag intakes.

"What the fuck!" I wanted to tell him but it came out as, "What the...beer? Yah, I do sometimes. Don't you drink?" I asked.

"I don't," He replied naively.

I exclaimed to myself—why on earth was I with him! a hyper-boring boy with archaic philosophies. Nevertheless the best part was that he paid the bills even after I insisted to do the same. Thank god! It soon got dark and we had to leave for home. I felt indebted and wanted to buy something for him, but what could I? May be some sweets!

"I take *paan*," He said as if it was a grand thing. I bought a packet of cigarettes for myself and two *paans* for us. He continued with his useless rambling making the way back home a tedious affair. The beer too, didn't work well.

From what I could discern from his ramblings, Hari's father, Rudra Hari was the youngest among the three brothers. The family had been fractioned due to some property dispute and there was nothing smooth in their brotherly relationship. Rudra Hari was close with his eldest brother, Dhruva Hari and communicated only with him. Dhruva's family had permanently settled in America after his son Vivek's *misadventure* with Catherine, an American.

Vivek, a Software engineer, had got a job in the US and was now married to Catherine. He had met her while pursuing engineering in Delhi. She had come to India to learn Indian Classical music. Their apartments were close by and they met one another quite often. Once Catherine fell seriously sick and Vivek had *nursed* her; the American had got her Indian classical *degree*.

Hari's own brother, Kirtan had died during the famous 1999 Kargil war between India and Pakistan. His uncle had insisted Hari's father to join them in the U.S. and get settled there but he had declined the offer due to the ailing health of his father, Shree Shree Narhari Prasad. Hari's other two uncles had permanently settled in Assam, a northeastern

Indian state after the historical exodus of the Nepalese being driven out of Meghalaya, another northeastern state.

As I reached my grandpa's place I told Hari it was time to part.

"Oh! Yes your house has come," He said gaily.

"You want to come?" I said out of obligation and in fact, knowing the response.

"No I am getting late. Will come some day later," He replied.

This was our first meeting and indeed not a pleasant one. Yet the day marked the beginning; the beginning of lasting camaraderie. I had never imagined I would be writing the story of a person who had bored me enough even to consider for a second meet.

*

Few days later, my grandma came with the news that somebody had come to see me.

I have two grandmas. My grandfather must have been a handsome hunk during his time. Even in his old age he carried his dignity and his words were the verdict especially to my two grandmas. It always occurred to me as if serving him was their *dharma*. What always flummoxed me was not only the extent of their devotion and care they showered on my grandpa but also the feeling of comradeship between them. I hardly remember the two fighting with each other or even with their 'hero' husband. Also they had seven children and it was only years later after my grandpa's death, did I know which child belonged to which mother. This aspect of my grandpa I really admire. My grandmas on the other hand were just concerned about my grandpa; taking care of his small needs and priorities. And, they have always been great cooks. Given that my parents allowed, I would always have had my food at my grandparents' place.

It was a day well begun for me until I discovered to my utter dismay that the news she had come with was indeed a 'breaking' one – Hari had come to see me! My grandma served us hot tea, *paranthas* and mixed curry which we thoroughly enjoyed and relished.

We met quite often after that and I gradually started to get the hang of him and understand him better. I realized that though he was utterly out of date and uninteresting, he had something which very few people have. He was different, though in a very odd way. He was a selfless soul who would do anything for nothing! He was an open book as the proverb goes, very fragile and vulnerable to exploitation. I had asked him one day,

"Why are you always so keen on helping others when they do not return your favors? People may use you to their advantage you know!"

To this Hari had answered, "You see I know people take advantage of me and according to you they use me, but I don't mind, at least I am useable to them. It's better than being useless," A prolonged pause in my thinking ended up in an abrupt smile.

Hari went on, "We can choose to see the world we want to, but this vision is determined by our conscience; that conscience which we justify. Just be good and the whole world will seem good to you."

Then if I could, I would tuck him and his philosophy into a polythene and garbage it into a dustbin. More so I would re-cycle it adding loads of practical wisdom as the chief ingredient and put it right back into his utopian head. But somewhere down the line some of his philosophies were epigrammatic; they definitely had some essence though it made no sense to me then.

Depth of some words are only realized when time itself seems to run short of it... Some words make no sense when one receives them with an outraged disposition but they function as an antidote to calm yourself down in seclusion.

Chapter II

May Fly

A very idiosyncratic aspect about Darjeeling hills is that the school level education is one of the best you can ever find. Perhaps it's the courtesy of the British or it could be something else. Nonetheless, schools here are really good. As such we have students flooding here not only from other states but also from nearby countries such as Nepal, Bhutan, Bangladesh, Thailand and so on...guarantying hefty donations. And thanks to the school benches too who eye such bounties. However, this should in no way dim the brightness of quality education provided by them along with the government and missionary schools in the locale.

Yet the fallacy of the place remains the lack of educational institutions at the higher level, thanks to the *relentless and sincere concern* of state and local authorities. This urges the elite Darjeeling denizens to send their wards mostly to Delhi, Bangalore or Kolkata with a self proclaimed promise in their hearts to mould them as technocrats, bureaucrats, doctors, engineers and of course entrepreneurs. Some however, owing to its proximity choose Siliguri.

I studied for my graduation from City College at Siliguri, a cosmopolitan town situated at the fringes of Darjeeling hills and wedged between three international South Asian borders of Nepal, Bhutan and Bangladesh. A chicken neck region of the northeastern India, Siliguri remains a gateway for trade, commerce and education for all inhabitants along its adjoining periphery.

I was sharing a flat with some more students from the hills who were studying in different colleges in Siliguri. Life was fun and the studies funnier. The crowd in the flat was a peculiar bunch of jostlers and every minute of life spent seemed special. Wangdi, my flat mate studied with me in the same college and Sashil, Sudhan, Millen, Mingma and Bristrit studied in the other colleges within the town. Studies were seldom a priority. We were more into music than into academics, not to mention a determined group of volleyball and football freaks that we were. It was like we had taken a long vacation to some far off exotic destination crammed with smoke, booze and music. We even formed a band and called ourselves 'Mayfly', the logic being living our lives to the fullest in a very short span of time, an allegory to the mayfly insect whose adult life spans up to three minutes to hardly a few days. We were just a carefree bunch trying every possible way to enjoy our initial step towards youth-hood. Everything seemed reachable and within our grasp. We were confident, free and we felt like lions in our own jungle.

*

A late night party had made me sleep till late in the morning only to miss my morning classes. A call in my cell phone woke me up.

"Hello," I said.

"Hi, man actually I called to inform you that I have decided to pursue my further studies in Siliguri."

It was Hari. I replied with ecstasy,

"Wow! That's great but as far as I remember you had plans to go to Bangalore."

"That, I'll tell you later. But I have one request to make."

"What is it tell me."

"Can I stay with you while I search for an accommodation? Actually my parents want me to stay with my father's friend's daughter, Deepa who is now married and settled at Siliguri, but I feel awkward."

"Come on man! Why do you have to search for accommodation or stay somewhere else when I am here? And you don't have to be so formal ok! Just come over."

"Yeah! But you aren't staying alone. I was apprehensive as to how your roommates will take to my joining in."

"Don't worry about that. They know you, I have talked a lot about you and you can stay with us permanently. In any case we were thinking of shifting to another building as the room rent has gone up lately. So your coming will be a boon for us," I said in a jovial manner.

"Ok thanks. But please seek their permission first," He stressed.

"Sure! By the way when are you planning to come?"

"Tomorrow itself, will it be fine?" He asked.

"Of course," I replied promptly and continued, "But when you come just visit my home. I will ask my mom to send me some money and bamboo shoot pickle."

"Sure," He said. I gave him the details of my location—78 *Shanti More, Sondeshpolly, Hakimpara, Macherhaat*, Siliguri.

In the evening I informed my friends about Hari's joining in to which they agreed unanimously.

*

It was about twelve the next day when he called me to inform that he was in a rickshaw and there had been a confusion about my address at *Macherhaat*. I immediately asked him to hand over the phone to the *rickshaw-wala* and directed him to my location in my broken Bengali. I went downstairs to receive him.

Few moments later I saw him and waved at him.

He got down and handed a fifty Rupee note to the *rickshaw-wala*.

The *rickshaw-wala* immediately prepared to leave. I intercepted him.

"Give him back his thirty rupees."

"*Hobae na*, we have already made a deal," He replied rudely.

"But the fare from Panitanki More to Shanti More is just twenty rupees. Why are you charging him more? You people see a 'hill face' and your greed instantly ignite, isn't it?"

New people are always open to con. The scene got heated and Hari sensing it said,

"Just leave it man. By taking thirty rupees more he won't become rich and I won't become poor, but may be his family will have something special with that money."

Yet again I bowed down to his absurdities.

On our way up to our flat I asked him,

"How come you suddenly changed your decision?"

"Actually she also has taken admission in Siliguri," He smiled as he said this.

"Oh I see, now I understand. You are still the Romeo you used to be huh!" Hari kept smiling.

"Do you know where has she taken her admission?" I asked.

"It's some Institute related to Technology."

"Oh! It's Siliguri Institute of Technology."

"Yap! That might be the one."

We entered our flat and I introduced Hari to my roommates. Everyone was more excited about the things he had brought along rather than meeting him. Apart from a parcel from my home, he had brought vegetables from his farm and also some boiled *simal tarul*, *samosas*, and of course a few packets of cigarettes. Hari had immediately struck the chord, and he became a darling when he declared that he would also buy us beer.

Post party, we had gone to bed rather late. I could not sleep and somehow started recapitulating about Hari and his first romance with Kavita.

As he had come he had seen and conquered!

Chapter III

Romeogiri

It was somewhere around 2002, the time when I had come back after my first year exams for a two month vacation. It was then I had visited his home and he had asked me for an unexpected favor. He wanted me to find out the name of the girl he had fallen for.

"Since when?" I had asked him.

"About six months," Hari blushed.

To my further enquiry he revealed that she lived in a village nearby.

"Come on she stays in a village close to ours and you don't even know her name? That is just absurd!" I lamented.

With certain hesitation and desperation I continued, "But, why do you need me to find out her name?"

"Because I can't ask her in person, I become as dead as a stone when I see her," This reply made me laugh innately. I was losing my patience but I assured,

"Okay, don't worry; I'll get her name for you."

My responsibility then was to find out everything I could about this girl and immediately report to Hari without keeping any information to myself.

I was curious to know about his love story and had asked him.

Their first encounter was on their way back home from school. As he was returning, a *Maruti Omni* van just passed by boarded with few school children which stopped at a distance not far away. There was a girl at the window side and she was looking straight at him. In one awkward moment, their eyes met. When the van went off he realized that he might have been wrong; the girl might not have looked at him after all. He looked around but found himself alone in that otherwise busy street which made him feel good. It was only after a few days of observation did Hari realize that she was for sure '*giving him the looks*', the thunderstruck of romance, you know!

Since then they started exchanging *looks* regularly, resulting in the alteration of Hari's school timings. Love is a catalyst of every routine, it changes from nowhere to everywhere, from person to timings. His everyday routine was reshuffled. He would wait for her to come, dressed in his own best possible way. After my insistence he had finally started applying hair-gel, which would prove instrumental in sharpening his side-locks. He would iron his uniform, take hours to get ready, and would be there at least half an hour before her arrival. They would exchange looks from their respective stationary positions until the vehicle would come and take her to school.

He would be on his way as soon as the students started boarding the cab which would hardly take five minutes. The cab would soon leave and she would pass him a smile as it gathered speed. It had many stoppages not in much distance from each other. Hari just prayed that on another stoppage, the one boarding from there would take just a little more time allowing him to sneak by the car; she would see him and smile discreetly. Then again she would overtake him and pass him with another smile. That smile was enough to make Hari's day.

In the evening too, Hari would be among the first to come out of the school. He had stopped waiting for his friends. He would hurriedly take a shortcut and be there on the route wherein there was the possibility of seeing her. Once he arrived on that love route, so to say, he would give up on his marathon and opt for a stroll. Most of the times he would be on time; but sometimes he was either late or way ahead. When he was late it meant the end of *Romeogiri*, but on days he would reach earlier, he would wait at the tea shop, adjacent to my grandpa's house.

The tea shop was quite an attraction for the local folks. It had four bamboos as its pillars; irregular in shape and size, strong enough to support its tin ceiling which was covered with plastic sheets that barely sheltered its owner and his customers during a down pour. The walls were constructed with broad wooden planks that were not sawed to perfection. They were nailed to the four pillars with very long nails, imperfectly bent at the exterior. Yet it stood like a fortress, providing its possessor with his means of sustenance. He was a jolly fellow in his forties and as a popular *chaiwala* he had probably served a million cups of tea so far. He had perfected the art of making tea and it really had a taste that couldn't be found anywhere else—Darjeeling tea mixed with his brilliance. Hari was his latest patron.

Hari's love interest would get down in front of the tea shop and clumsily stroll by. Hari would follow her. However, her younger sister's constant company was a hindrance for him to initiate any conversation.

*

Her name was Kavita. That, I found out by the location of her house he had given me; not at all a difficult task; it was only for the idiot that he was. The next day I gave him his most awaited trophy, her name.

Kavita hailed from Mirik, a lake town sub-division in Darjeeling. She had been staying at her distant relative's house as a paying guest. She had stayed out of her hometown for many years while studying in Delhi and had returned home that year, still choosing to study outside.

"Now what Hari! Need I do something more?" I asked.

"Not really," He simply said.

"Nothing! You are gonna live with just her name?" I exclaimed.

There was no answer. His eyes were just roving around, trying hard to avoid my surprised stare.

I was concerned, so I suggested, "Why don't you propose to her?"

"I can't. Actually I have been trying to propose since months but have failed. I wait for her cab every day. I hurriedly come to the place where she gets down and I always try to tell her how much I love her. But my courage always belies me. What do I do?"

I couldn't digest so I said, "What's so difficult in saying 'I love you'? Be a man. Go up to her and let her know how you feel about her."

"It's easier said than done," He had replied.

Eventually, I coaxed him to start the conversation with her. The next day he was to make the first move. I remember telling him one particular line in our vernacular that night, "*valae nai baasnu parcha, pothi baascha kahilae?*" — meaning it's always the rooster that crows and not the hen.

He would lie in the bed and finally, with daylight, he would go to sleep. After all, he said to himself, it is probably only insomnia. Many must have it – Ernest Hemingway

Chapter IV

The Verbal Encounter

Sometimes it's better just to let your steps lead the path rather than searching for the route.

The next day we were waiting for her to come. She finally did. I had never seen her in person but I could tell by her appearance that it was Kavita, since Hari had so intricately described her. Her hair was coal black and ended just a few inches below her chin. It suited her small round face and as the morning sun rays fell lightly on her head it shone like some kind of metal, finely polished. Her skin was fair and clear and her dark brown eyes had some kind of intensity, some kind of curiosity. Without moving her head, her eyes would survey all the possible angles. It was as if she was always ready for some sudden or abrupt attack.

"Hari, go and talk to her. What are you waiting for? The cab will be here any time," I said. He did not budge.

He was feeling very nervous, I could sense but I kept on pestering him. I literally pushed him towards her direction. She sensed what he was up to and was excited and nervous at the same time, but probably less than him, I assumed. I was watching them and he literally staggered as if his legs were shackled. I had a gut feeling that he would spoil it all and he didn't prove me wrong. Out of sheer nervousness he swerved to the left and instead of going towards her, went to a shop nearby and pretended to buy something. By then the van had already arrived and when all were seated, it whizzed by in no time. Hari came back restraining his smile with the tongue between his teeth. I showed him my fist and air punched him at his frivolity. Seeing the disappointment plastered all over my face he put his hands in his pocket and shrugged. He had completely botched up what would have been a momentous morning. He had bought some pencils instead, poor Romeo!

"Why on earth did you have to buy pencils?" I pounced back, "Didn't you find anything interesting?"

As usual he would simply say, "Man, I was really nervous, didn't know what to do." "Since a kid at the shop was asking for a pencil, I bought it too." Then we couldn't help but laugh. But he promised he would definitely make the move in the evening. And promises for Hari were not meant to be broken.

In the evening we both perched ourselves at the tea shop. Meanwhile I was continuously drip-feeding him about the things he should be saying and asking. He was still in his school uniform. I was thinking how he would approach her; whether he would spoil it once again and things alike. She finally came and passed us by. Hari followed her and I followed them.

He trudged towards her and uttered, "Excuse me, may I know your name?"

"Yeah, but why?" She said with a mischievous smile.

"Just like that," He replied with composure. But beneath the calm exterior he was definitely exploding.

"It's Kavita," She said in an amiable voice.

"Pardon!" said he just to hear the melody of her voice again. She repeated her name.

"Hi! I am Hari," was all he could utter.

He knew that his arsenal of words which I had armored him with had all dried up. He wouldn't be able to say anything. He walked alongside for a while and when he couldn't make a conversation he stopped midway and abruptly turned back, without giving her any clue as to why he wanted to know her name. It was obvious that she knew why but even with her readiness of sudden attacks, this one was completely different. She kept strolling away without even looking back. He made a mess of it once again. Nevertheless, that was his first verbal encounter with her.

*

From then on, the regular exercise of greeting her on the way to school just geared up, and gradually everyone boarding the cab including the driver knew about the chemistry that was building up between the two. In fact, the driver seemed to like Hari. He would often talk to Hari from his driver's seat so that Hari and Kavita could exchange looks—more looks. Hari was on cloud nine.

Life is beautiful when you fall in love. Out of nowhere you seem to grow wings and begin to fly high in ecstasy. Everything was perfect for him and I could sense his excitement. I remember him thanking me time and again to the point of getting me irritated. But I was happy for him. We decided that he would propose to her and I happily offered myself as the medium—a post perfect boy. He handed me the stuff that I was supposed to deliver. I advised him to ventilate his feelings verbally but he opted for the traditional way of dealing things. A card and a letter was his choice.

The letter had long been written. The red envelope had started to wear off a trifle and the constant fiddling had dirtied it on the sides. I told him that it would be delivered the very next day. I took the letter with the card clumsily tucked into the same envelope. My curiosity made me open the envelope and read its content.

"Dear Kavita,

I have been seeing you for quite some time now and every time I see you I can't help falling in love with you. I don't know what this feeling is but what I know is that, this is the first time it has ever happened to me and I know that it's for real. We may exchange looks, but I don't know what place I occupy there in your heart, so just wanted to know your feelings towards me. Do you love me? And more importantly will you be my girlfriend? Please reply as soon as possible, will be eagerly waiting for your reply.

Hari"

*

I met her alone the next day. She must have recognized me but still I said, "Excuse me, I am Hari's friend. He has asked me to deliver this to you," I handed her the envelope.

"Oh! But what is it?" She asked with her prepared curiosity.

"You check it for yourself," I said.

She took it promptly and put it in her bag.

"Thank you," She said and left.

It was the first time I had seen and observed her from such proximity. She looked really beautiful with a lovely pair of eyes well complemented by her fair skin and a slim figure. She seemed less alarmed today. Maybe she was expecting some kind of intercession from Hari after that unusual evening. Her eyes were not wavering but had a sparkle and her nasal voice had an air of poise in it.

Later, when I informed Hari about our meeting he was 'happily nervous'. What would her reply be? She didn't seem to be going around with someone else. Maybe she too liked him or, maybe not. He slept a sleepless night.

> *The oldest and strongest emotion of mankind is*
> *fear, and the oldest and the strongest kind of fear*
> *is the fear of the unknown – H.P. Lovecraft*

Chapter V

Limbo

Next day we waited for her response. As always Hari was early. But she didn't turn up and guess what! Hari didn't go to school. This was one of the conventions he had established for himself. I had asked him the reason. The *Romeo* in a somber mood had replied, "I will at least be close to her." What could I possibly say to such absurdities? The next day we repeated the same procedure and she didn't turn up again. The convention continued, wasting another page from his school diary *imprinting* reasons for his casual leave.

However, to our relief the cab driver signaled Hari to come and handed him an envelope. We wasted no time in unveiling it. There was a letter and a card. Hari read the letter and his mood turned grey. He passed it to me; she had written,

"Dear Hari,

I am sorry I can't accept your proposal. Actually I come from a very strict family and I can't dare to be in a relation. I personally think that we would look better as friends than anything more. And one more thing please don't talk to me when I am with my sister. Last time when you asked me my name she complained it to my relatives and I had a tough time. But don't worry I handled it. But we can talk when I am alone. You can also write to me whenever you feel like. And please don't take my reply otherwise; it's not that I don't like you. I do, it's just that I don't love you.

'Pal to Remain'

Kavita"

I couldn't comprehend the reply but I had to make him realize that the situation was not as bad as he would have imagined.

Girls are really hard to decipher. You never know what runs in their mind. From the things that were obvious to me, she was in love with him. In fact, it was she who had initiated the spark in his heart and now she was playing it cool. He was very upset, he didn't go to school that day and I chose to stay with him. I stayed with him that night too. There was a frigid atmosphere in the room; we basically sat in a gloomy silence.

In reality this isn't a big deal, but for a novice like Hari, it indeed was.

"Hari I think you should take it slow," Said I, "Can't you be friends for now; know each other a little bit more and then commit. You never know whether she is your type or not."

He said nothing. We had our dinner in the room itself. Throughout dinner he had his eyes lowered, he didn't talk much. In bed, I could sense he was sobbing discreetly and I pretended to fall asleep. I felt no words could console him. He had just fallen from his mountain of hopes to a pit of despair. When I woke up at five in the morning, he was awake. Probably, he didn't sleep that night; his bleary red eyes were a testimony of his desperation. Meanwhile, a plan had been cooking up in my head which I thought could just bring things to normal. So I said,

"Listen Hari, I think you should not see her for a week at least."

He gave a frazzled look and replied after a momentary silence, "But it will be difficult for me."

"Man! I know girls much better than you. You know what their biggest weakness is? Its curiosity, and if you can arouse it, many things can be done. So trust me and do as I say; believe me, I want your good," I asserted.

Initially he hesitated, but then finally agreed and changed his timings completely as directed by me. He did not wait for her anymore and went to his school way ahead of her. He was no more a patron at the tea shop.

*

A week later Hari came to my house in an elated mood to tell me that my strategy had paid off. She had sent him a letter. Not only that a small teddy bear with one of its eyes in a permanent blink came as a gift. There seemed no boundary to Hari's happiness.

Hari let me read the letter:

"Dear Hari,

Hi! Wats up? I don't know from where to start and how. Ok let me come to the point. I don't see you these days and I know why you are doing this. I know my reply has hurt you. But I can't be in a relation as I have other important things to live up to. But I don't want you to act as a stranger or go away from my life. In fact, I always want you to be by my side helping me, guiding me, scolding me when I am wrong, accompanying me when I am lonely; a person whom I would want there always with me. But I also feel that it is not the right time to get into relationships. I don't think we are mature enough to decide on all these things. And let me tell you that there is no one else in my life. And even if I get engaged with anyone, it will be after I finish my schooling. I know I am sounding boring but that's the real 'me'. Also know that all these days when I didn't see you, I missed you. You were always there in my prayers and my mind. If you care for me please don't do this. I really need you but I can't be in a relation as I have problems of my own. I swear in God's name that I am not lying. I don't know what your feelings towards me will be after reading this letter. But for me you are always going to remain near and dear. But even after telling you all this, if you still don't turn up tomorrow, I will think that you don't love me.

Kavita"

The letter was replete with vagueness but one thing was clear that now she did feel for him and had started to miss him. From the very next day he repeated his old schedule following the vague line of his first love life. When it's neither completely 'yes' nor completely 'no' you can understand the limbo situation that one is in.

But the problem with them was the most obvious one, 'communication gap'. They hardly spoke even though they went to their schools 'almost' together. Even on weekends, it was only with her aunt that she went out. She was too scared to meet and he was too much of a coward then, to call her up.

*

Once I had asked, "Why don't you call her when she has given you her phone number?"

"Man, her relatives are strict and it's always her aunt who picks up the call. I think if I call, she might have to face problems at home," He explained.

"Come on you can't love and be scared at the same time."

"No it's not about getting scared; it's just that I don't want her to get into trouble because of me."

I really can't justify his feelings nor understand them completely. What I can presume is that he was too utopian in his approach towards love and it was not going to do him good. May be he knew that he was going nowhere and that their relation had no base at all. He was helpless, tired and a bit irritated with this sort of life. Yet he endured his pain with stoicism. On top of that he did crazy stuffs. He would constantly go to a Kali temple which was about an hour and a half away from our village, just to bring her blessed flowers during her exams. This he did without fail.

He would get up very early in the morning; take a shower and literally run to be able to arrive back before she left for her school. Sometimes such deeds of his amused me and sometimes it pissed me off. He would do numerous other things for the one with whom his relationship wasn't clear and his goodness in this matter really surprised me. My point is that any un-conditionality is the first principle of love that I understand, but it has to be for the one who deserves it. Having said that how are we to know who is right and who is not?

Love is like a dictator who commands us to
do several things. Some turn out to be absurd,
some great and some, well... spiteful

Chapter VI

Those Days

It was already two in the morning and I hadn't found sleep yet. I got up and lit a cigarette. Then I thought the relationship between Hari and Kavita was ambiguous and vague and mostly haunted by communication gap. In majority of cases that I have seen, the most essential thing that keeps up a relation is communication. Some romantics may still believe in higher love, of love so everlasting and full of melancholy, drama and glory. But in reality we somehow fail to become that 'Romeo' or 'Juliet', because our heart needs that warmth when our beloved cuddles into our arms. Our eyes need to see them smiling back at us, making us know that they are happy. Our ears need to hear their voices, their laughter and their cries, giving us moments of joy and despair. How could one possibly choose to love someone for ages without even seeing or hearing or touching; when all of these are the pillars that hold the thing called 'Love'.

Communication gap was a pertinent factor even in our relationship. Those days mobile phone was a luxury which very few people could afford and we had to depend on the land line which most of the times would be answered by the elders. Moreover, privacy was not assured. Mobiles would become our necessity once we came out of our home town. Still the call rates were high and there was a charge levied even for 'incoming' calls. My parents however did buy me one just a week back, that too after much melodrama.

This is precisely why I was not able to contact him regularly and help him out. More importantly, I was unaware of the things that had happened between them since our last meeting. Poor Hari I thought, I would ask him about his love Kavita in detail the next morning and went off to sleep.

*

Next day was a Saturday, apparently a half day and for us it meant no classes. Soon the other band members, our friends would come and we would dedicate the whole day to music. Everyone woke up late except Hari. By the time we woke up Hari had already prepared tea and had also brought a large packet of 'Good Day' biscuits, a luxury we couldn't afford at the end of the month.

He brought me tea and biscuits and it was then I asked him about Kavita. From his accounts it was clear that their relationship didn't grow at all. I felt that the only thing which grew was his love or should I say his pain, a poor lovelorn! It seemed to me that their relationship was on the brink. Further, he also detailed me about how he had initially decided to go to Bangalore, one of the metropolitan cities in India and take up law but now under romantic circumstances he had instead chosen to pursue Sociology at Siliguri.

Soon our room was flooded with other friends, the musicians who stayed in and around had all gathered up. Marvin our backbone, the lead guitarist, and a versatile song writer/composer and Aakansha the main vocalist were giggling in the room. Reetesh who played the bass guitar and Aashish the drummer were arguing on some issues with Wangdi the Congo player and our keyboardist Sudhan. Sashil and I played the rhythm guitar for the band and Millen was our manager. We used to do a lot of covers. Some Led Zeppelin, Metallica, Megadeth, Black Sabbath, Dave Matthews, Pink Floyd etc. and it did sound well and tight. Mayfly would one day become great, that's what we thought but with our graduation, it started to fade into oblivion. Everyone had to make their career and thus ended the big fat Mayfly dream. Sometimes I wonder if we had chosen to make Mayfly our career where we would have ended—maybe a few Grammys, a few million dollars, fame and glory, world tours, beautiful girls throwing themselves upon us. Ah! It would have been great. But, it was not to be.

Hari soon acclimatized with my other friends and especially our peculiarities. He loved to listen us play and it influenced him so much that he started to take guitar lessons. He even bought a guitar.

Around that time, Bird Flu had caused quite a scare in Siliguri. I remember there were constant rumors of Bird Flu having spread all over West Bengal. People had stopped buying chicken and this proved a boon for us as the chicken price had hit an all time low. "Well, what the heck!" we thought, "A poor sick chicken couldn't possibly kill us."

We would live like kings at the beginning of the month. But as our pocket money would wane off with passing weeks, our royalty would taper down too. We would often talk about different meat recipes for hours but would end up eating rice with *alu ko charcharae* (miniature form of French fries) and *gunruk ko jhol* (Gorkha soup). When some relatives or parents would come for a visit, they used to bring for us our traditional Nepali delicacies like *Churpi* (Cheese) and *Kinema* (fermented soya bean). But such family visits would sometimes pose a problem and with it came a wave of 'never seen before' discipline among us. Everyone would be busy cleaning the rooms, desperately searching and throwing away the cigarette and *biri* buds and hiding the empty beer bottles.

Anything that gets your blood racing is probably worth doing – Hunter S. Thompson

Chapter VII

The Phone Call

Merely a week had passed when Hari received a call from an unknown number.

"Hello?" She said. Hari immediately recognized Kavita's voice. "Actually I got a cell phone yesterday so I called you up."

She went on, "I am in Siliguri and have taken admission in Siliguri Institute of Technology."

"I know that," He replied.

"Even I am in Siliguri. By the way where do you stay?" He asked.

"In *Salbari*, and you?"

"*Shanti More.*"

"Oh! Then let's meet someday."

"Definitely," He replied.

After that morning, phone calls and text messages became a regular affair. Then the day for them to meet finally arrived.

He was excited. They decided to roam around *Bidhan* market together and that was how the romance had actually started.

Later that night we asked him about the day's happenings. Everyone was excited as I had told them about his little love story.

We also asked inappropriately, "How much did you finish today?"

"Twelve hundred only...for two plates of fish rice, ice cream, chocolates and she wanted to buy some earrings too," He grinned.

"With that amount we could have had luncheon for all of us," I said and we all laughed.

*

Their sporadic meetings gained regularity with the passage of time. Both began to give one another more time and there slowly developed warmth in their relationship. Kavita even shifted her room to the building wherein we were staying. Hari had proven that patience pays off. They started spending time in her room and kept chatting for hours. They began to lose track of time, engrossed in each other's company. Soon he started having dinner with her. Matters were progressing between them and both were feeling the same emotion of love this time. The sky was changing its color and far away Hari could see the rainbow shining bright.

Meanwhile we in the room had decided that we would do whatever it takes to help him out. Precisely for this reason we established good contacts with Kavita.

*

One night he entered the room in a stark mood of despair. To my enquiry he said something in a gibberish manner as if he didn't want to share the reason. I kept on staring at his painful eyes and he eventually erupted.

"Ah! She is getting a lot of proposals in her college, and I have no idea why on earth is she telling me about it!"

I could sense a hint of desperation and anguish in him. I understood what Kavita was actually hinting at but I decided to keep it to myself for a little longer just to relish his fretfulness. To compound his misery further, I teased,

"So you feel jealous too!"

He gave a look filled with surging indignation. Then I thought any further delay in revealing Kavita's intentions would only fuel his rage further. Hence I asked him,

"What did she tell you?"

"She said she was not sure as to what should be done with those proposals," He contemplated with his eyes downcast.

"What was your answer?" I enquired further.

"Come on what could my answer be? I just advised her to do whatever she finds her happiness in," saying this he walked towards the balcony. It was then I shouted.

"You are such a fool you know, she wants you to propose to her, don't you even get that." At this he turned back from the altar of the door and came close to me. He grasped my arms and screamed in utter excitement,

"Really is that so? But she didn't tell me!" He said with his face radiating.

"You really are impossible. Dammit! You didn't even know that you were always at the altar of romance since the day she came to stay in this building. So my dear Harry make it fast or else some other guy will be the occupant of her heart and her room and you will be left drinking with us," I professed.

"So what do I do now?"

"Come on! Just propose to her... tomorrow itself," I stressed.

"But I need your help then."

"Let's do one thing. We will talk about it in detail in the evening with others."

He simply nodded in agreement.

I related Hari's intention to the rest in the evening. It was unanimously concluded that he should go ahead with the proposal. We sat in a circle with beer bottles in our hands, sponsored by Hari and laid down the blueprint thinking diligently about the intricacies involved in the proposal. We made him understand that every help would be possible from our side. That decisive night I made him clear that he should do it verbally and not resort to a card or a letter.

His anxiety wouldn't let him sleep. He knew he was a master in spoiling such occasions. He was shifting numerous positions and probably thought of a million words and ways to make his proposal.

> *The thought of tomorrow scares me…I wish*
> *I could prolong the night a little longer for I*
> *know not if it's a beginning or an end.*

Chapter VIII

Fool or No Fool

The anxious dawn had beckoned.

Hari went to her room and acted normal. He was to make his first move as we had already planned. He asked if she would like to go for a movie, to which she agreed.

Hari was least bothered with the drama that was unfolding on the white screen – those three hours seemed eternal to him. After the movie they went to a restaurant where Hari finally broke the ice,

"I need to ask you something."

Kavita impervious of it asked, "What is it?"

Hari looked straight into her deep contemplating eyes and finally uttered, "Would you like to spend the rest of your life with me?"

She said nothing but smiled and blushed. He felt his hands trembling; the silence was awkward and long; his throat went dry. He sipped some water and could hear his heart beat in a peculiar way. The waiter broke the frozen silence as he served the food in his specialized way and left. The silence once again enveloped the table until the dinner was over. He paid the bills and they came out. Silence continued even on their ride back home.

They reached her room and out of the blue Kavita took his hands into hers and said, "Hari I too love you a lot, a lot more than you know. But remember one thing, I love my parents more than I love you and if ever a day comes when I need to choose between you and my parents I shall choose them and if such a situation confronts you, I would want you to do the same."

This was I thought a unique kind of answer and a strange way of saying 'yes' to the one you are in love with. Sometimes perhaps, incongruities remain unexplained in the realm of love.

Kavita continued, "I feel proud to be yours and you know what impressed me the most is the fact that we used to spend so much of time together, at times till late at night, yet you never took advantage of the situation." She hugged him with a kiss and uttered those magical words "I love you" yet again. He felt as if he had just been conferred a knighthood.

That night they chatted as if it was the first time. It was the usual talk but today the difference was that she was nestling in his arms oblivious to the world around.

*

When he came to the room it was already three in the morning. He couldn't control the excitement and kept smiling to himself. He could feel his blood rush to the cheeks and ears. He was on seventh heaven and wanted to share it with us but there we lay, like stone sculptures chiseled by some great sculptor ever to remain motionless, probably dreaming our own dreams. I remember it was 15 March 2003, a momentous day for Happy Hari. He would have desperately wanted to reveal his happiness, dance to his amazement or sing his laughter out because he was now finally successful in his love. But poor Hari had none to share his elation. He tried to wake us but neither of us budged. He couldn't sleep that night and nor could she.

Finally, the sleeping giants woke up. The weary sun had just let its rays travel through space to reach that part of our sleepy world, and in that instance Hari had finished telling us his last night's tale. When all of us met for breakfast in the morning, loads of accolades were savored on the victorious knight for his long awaited accomplishment.

"I am very happy today guys. What do you want for a treat? Tell me," He said.

"Right now, another cup of tea would be better," I said.

"*Jaar,*" screamed Marvin, he had stayed with us.

Hari smiled and disappeared into the kitchen singing some romantic song and after a few minutes came back with a tray full of tea cups and biscuits.

It was celebration time. Hari was happy to treat us again and this time, a special dinner accompanied with '*kodo ko jaar*'. *Jaar* is a typical Nepali alcoholic beverage prepared by fermenting whole grain millet. It is served in a feet tall jar called *Tongba*, made of a large and solid piece of Himalayan bamboo. Nowadays, even long plastic or metal jars are used as *Tongba*. Hot water is poured to the brim and left for about five minutes and then sipped through a straw called *Pipsing* made of thin hollow bamboo which is punctured at one end that acts as a filter. The taste is quite extraordinary. Nothing beats the feel of sipping the heavenly hot water mixed with the trippy fermented millet juice through the *Pipsing*.

After breakfast, Sudhan and Wangdi went to our regular Bhutia restaurant at *Salugara* and bought ten kilos of *jaar* and eight *Pipsings*. Since we didn't have *Tongbas*, we put half of the *Jaar* in a bathroom bucket which Sashil had hardly washed and the boiled water poured from the top made the millet dangerously slushy, enough to put many down to their knees. Eight *Pipsings,* now ready for the sip in the same bucket including Hari this time. The jubilation was definitely inexplicable for Hari in his maiden experience of sipping the *kodo ko jaar*. We were determined to make him high and it would certainly not be his last; that we would ensure. The party went on at his *cost*.

*

Months passed and their relation strengthened with each passing day. Now he spent all his time with her and literally became a tourist in his own room. He would often come to the room with stuffs, mostly the edibles, given by her and we would devour it in no time. However, he made it a point to keep the wrappers intact for some utopian reasons. Sometimes she would make delicacies for him, especially *alu parantha*, his favourite. When such specialties were on the menu, he would inform us. We would then go one by one to her room, first me looking for Hari, then Sudhan for me and eventually we would all be there getting a taste of the *paranthas*. Later Kavita understood our hide and seek strategy and the amount of delicacies also increased. Wow! For us but very soon to our dismay the trend of common mess with mouth watering delicacies simply disappeared.

Our days at the end of the month would be in impoverished condition. We couldn't even afford cigarettes and lunch was a far cry. On such occasions we would empty the ashtray and reignite the leftover buds. Our talks would revolve around Hari and what he might be doing in her room and most importantly what he ate. Sometimes we went to her room just to disturb them. She out of obligation would be forced to make tea and would offer some biscuits or some other snacks probably hoping for us to leave at the earliest.

*

Once he came from her room at three in the morning. I was up as I had some assignments to complete. He didn't expect me to be awake that late and became nervous as he saw me and immediately went to his bed. As he walked past me, his body reeked of a feminine perfume. I observed him closely and his lips bore a faint residue of gloss which he must have encroached.

"You kissed her?" I asked.

He didn't utter anything for a while. He slowly lay back on the bed, clasped his hands behind his head and kept staring at the ceiling. He was probably thinking whether he should tell me or not. He would never hide anything from me. I had a feeling that he didn't want to share it with me as he might have thought that I would think badly of her. Poor Hari, I knew well enough to con things out of him even if he declined to share.

"Tell me man. Something happened today eh! Go on, I won't tell anyone. I promise," I insisted.

Then, quite awkwardly but specifically he started to reveal what had happened between them. I kept listening very eagerly and without saying a word. He knew he shouldn't be saying and I knew I shouldn't be hearing but we kept our guilt aside and decided to *share* it anyway.

That very night Kavita insisted him to stay with her and this would be their first night stay together. It had been drizzling outside and the night was chilly. Darkness coupled with the rain was making the atmosphere romantically sensuous. Moreover, he was sleeping with a girl for the first time in his life. He was feeling strange and was experiencing a feeling that was alien to him. With her touch and her breath close by, he could sense a sudden rush of blood within him. He kissed her gently. He seemed to know the art well. He then remembered his first kiss which he had completely messed up with. But now it was different. He kissed her neck and could feel the warmth of her bosoms. In her extreme excitement she murmured something in his ears. He couldn't hear her properly and asked her what she meant. She moaned, "Make love to me."

He was taken aback by her words as he was not expecting it to go that far.

"But I don't have protection."

"Doesn't matter just do it," She demanded.

He in an instance withdrew himself from her and said, "Look dear we shouldn't go that far. Please try to understand, this is not the right time."

She was breathing heavily and her expression had changed drastically. She was blushing as if gallons of blood had just been injected to her face.

"This is not right…will you be able to face your parents after this!" He said and reached out for her.

She shrugged her shoulders as he touched her and said, "Don't touch me, please don't touch me."

"Why?" He asked.

"You won't understand," Was the reply.

She got down from the bed, folded her legs and covered it with her hands and sat there for a while. He went closer, emulated her position and smiled at her.

She with a firm voice said, "Don't smile and don't look at me."

He didn't want to enrage her further so he just sat behind her. After a while he got up and said that he was leaving for his room and asked her to lock up the door.

After hearing his story I said, "If it would have been me, I would have immediately made love to her, good enough for her to remember for a long, long time!"

"Please don't say like that. I love her so much and I have never thought things that way. For me love is only about emotions and feelings and nothing else," He twitched.

"You are a naive, a forlorn fool," Said I and shifted my position in order to sleep.

"A fool or no fool brother, I don't regret for what I did," Said Hari.

Passion is universal humanity. Without it religion, history, romance and art would be useless – Honore de Balzac

Chapter IX

Divine Bewilderment

One early night he came to me and said, "Hey man I need to talk to you."

"What is it about?" I asked.

"Actually I am having a strange feeling since a week now. I want to make things right between Kavita and me. I want to make love to her. Should I?" He asked.

I was surprised but I understood it and said, "It's perfectly ok since you love each other so much. In fact it will make your love stronger."

"Is it so?" He exclaimed. "But, how?" was his innocent query.

"Look I don't have time to explain all this. So just do it and you'll know it for yourself. But be safe or very soon we might have a junior Harry," I teased.

"But I feel… feel awkward to buy it," Hari stammered.

"Then ask one of our guys, they may be having," I suggested.

"Then everyone will come to know about it. They will think ill of her. Moreover they treat her like their sister; it will make both of them awkward when they face each other the next time. Please help," He pleaded.

"Come on there is no big deal here every one will understand. In fact, no one believes that you two have not made love yet. You are mostly in her room and you still worry about what others think? It's not necessary that people think the way you do. Just ask from them nothing will happen. Even they make love to their girlfriends, it's all right, okay!" I said with obvious emphasis.

He kept silent; I could sense the awkwardness he was feeling; so I continued, "And if you don't want to do that, then go to a medical store somewhere far from our place and just ask for a packet, no one will kill you," I said with desperation.

"Man, I really can't. Please do something," He pleaded.

"What?" I demanded.

Hari shyly uttered, "Brother please buy one for me, I will not need the entire packet," I had no reply to this.

Actually, I myself feel a little awkward buying a protection. It does feel like a self proclamation! Nonetheless, I went to the market and bought a packet for him.

*

Next morning Hari expressed his desire to Kavita and they decided to stay together for the night. Making love for the first time is a difficult task and in Hari's case it was no better.

He kissed her intensely. His hands unrobed her gently. Her slender body in complete beauty stood in front of him and his wildness knew no boundary. He described about how he had placed himself between her legs in a very discomfited manner and very awkwardly said, "I don't know where" and she guided him through. He could feel his manhood throb as if it had a heart of its own. With yearn of warmth and love together, they were finally inside each other. Cuddled together they became one—one soul.

Unknown avenues have always attracted humans since time immemorial and the ones who enter are not left without being caught up in bewilderment. Some experiences are disturbing while some are heavenly; Hari's experience sounded magnificent.

Start by doing what's necessary, then do what's possible, and suddenly you are doing the impossible – Francis of Assisi

Chapter X

The Kalimpong Carnival

Independence Day celebration in Kalimpong is second to none in terms of grandeur, vigor and intensity. The day beckons an air of festivity. It's not just a festival, but a carnival that lasts for two *eventful* days. It is often contended that it parallels the 26 January Republic Day celebration in New Delhi.

The schools around Kalimpong start their parade practice, musical band troops, drill and other sports activities from the month of July itself. The venue being the 'Mela ground', thousands of people from everywhere throng to witness the celebration. The inhabitants around the town are quick to occupy the front seats, leaving rest of the seats in the gallery for late comers. Many seats are booked in advance by placing of handkerchiefs, umbrellas and even sacks. The owners come and occupy the seats much before the celebration begins. Brawl and arguments over the seats are a common sight as people have to prove rightful ownership of the placed objects.

Hari was for the first time celebrating the Independence Day with his girl and was really excited. He had occupied a second row seat in the gallery for them. Hari had been careful enough to occupy a seat near the exit stairs, so that later in between he could easily sneak out around the town and enjoy other festivities with Kavita.

It's amazing to see how all schools come up with such wonderful participations every year. There are separate prizes for the winners of the parade and also for the top three bands. The prize is not that of cash but of glory, a cup which everyone would like to get their hands on to. Thus, the schools try to come up with something extra, something unique and something different every year.

Slowly the schools, one by one march their parade, armored with sophisticated band troops. The parades pass through the *Gandhi gate* and halt in the part of the ground allotted to them. There is an announcer on an elevated stage announcing the arrival of the schools and also giving inputs about the Gorkha freedom fighters who have laid down their lives for the Indian independence. Slowly and steadily the ground begins to fill up. All the schools having marked their arrival, the chief guest hoists the tricolor, followed by the national anthem, the tune of which was composed by a fellow Nepali legend Ram Singh Thakuri. The audience rise up and sing the anthem with pride—thereby asserting their *Indian-ness* so loosely attached in the country. After the speeches of few eminent personalities of the town, the parade marches out, displaying their best as it is then that their performance will be adjudged by the jury. As they approach the chief guest's dais they offer their salute to the flag of honor which is acknowledged by the chief guest with reverence. When all the schools mark their exit; the floor is open for other competitions.

Strange things happen on this day. In one past instance, Kumudini Homes, a renowned school in town, had refrained from participating in the event. The reason being, the chief guest then had acknowledged their salute with a hand in his pocket. Kumudini Homes later participated in the Independence Day celebration after a good three years' gap. Thanks to those numerous requests from different people and corners. However, when they actually participated, they had sent around a thousand of students for the parade competition, thereby making the ground congested. Since then the limit had been fixed to three hundred. Hari and Kavita were nostalgic witnessing the parade.

Kavita expressed her desire to have *puchka*. They decided to sneak out after the parade got over. If the celebration inside is grand, the life outside the ground is all the more charming, more alluring. The roads are all jam-packed, hardly sparing any space for the pedestrians. Ever so silent Kalimpong suddenly moults into a hub of feverish activities. The town is festooned with different adornments and the colourful flags add to the gaiety of the occasion.

The *puchka* stalls put up by vendors from far and near were mostly surrounded by the female folk. One of such stalls was empty and the *puchka walla* too was missing. Hari and Kavita waited for a while and finally the vendor came mincing a pinch of tobacco between his index finger and the palm.

Hari exclaimed, "This *bhaiya* must have come from the toilet and is also preparing *khaini*. Do you still want to have it?"

"*Chhya...*" said she and punched him in his arm. "*Puchka* is *puchka* and you have not seen this *bhaiya* coming out of a toilet. So pleaseeee Hari let me enjoy my *puchkas*," Said Kavita and started enjoying the chilly *puchkas*. Later she wanted to have *Fumbi*, a local favourite jelly like edible item primarily found in Kalimpong. It is made out of pulses, generally enjoyed with spicy chutney made up of groundnut or *Teel* and mixed with garlic and *dallae*.

It's business time for the hoteliers; and other petty business doers selling bright colored balloons, plastic toys and many more things to tempt small children who come from far and wide villages.

And for the youths the day is no less than another Valentine's Day; indeed a great opportunity for the 'singles' to 'mingle'.

It's also a time for 'fashion show'. In fact, many people get new outfits for Independence Day. This is how serious and ceremonious it gets in Kalimpong. But the picture in other sub-divisions is hardly that grand, in fact no other place in whole of the state or for that matter in the country itself can get grander than Kalimpong.

It is a dry day but ironically many are seen in a drunken state. More often there are brawls and fights for multiple reasons. The police also finally get to do their job.

The result on the first, second and third prize had been announced in all categories; parade, band and drill. There were cheers all around the ground and also on the streets. The declaration of results in the stadium was also being telecast in the television screens installed outside the shops for the occasion. And now it was time for the football final, the gala event of the day. However, only the two finals, the mini and the senior division at school level would be held that day. The grounds men would start the preparation for the most awaited moment.

That year two I.C.S.E (private) schools had reached the mini division finals; this rarely happens. It was to be played between St. Augustine School and Rockvale Academy. The ground soon would be flooded with their respective supporters. A peculiarity so idiosyncratic to the football viewing in Kalimpong is that, the schools come with all their bands and create new cheering slogans every year. Most of them are created keeping in mind who the opponent is. What I mean is; it is not only enjoyable to watch football but also to listen to the cheers.

The senior division match was the most awaited; it was to be held between not only the two heavy weights but also the arch rivals. It would be a India-Pakistan thriller, a match between Kumudini Homes and Scottish Universities Mission Institution (SUMI). Whenever the two collide, it is excitement guaranteed culminating into fights more often than not. Even the police security beefs up and surely it would that day. Even the old folks who had chosen to view the celebration at home would come out. All the charm now would lie in the ground; and the streets begin to sparse a bit, leaving only the love birds around. Some would even sacrifice their company for the match. In fact, the public want the two always in the finals but at times it doesn't happen, it disappoints them; most of them are alumni of one or the other. Nonetheless, they do turn up for the finals.

Hari and Kavita decided to skip the match. Now there were lesser people on the streets, others had been magnetized to the match. They went to a restaurant for a cup of coffee; after all, lovers have their own world.

Kuminidi Homes had scored a goal. Hari punched the air. A little later the news spread that the score had been equalized and it was Kavita's turn to celebrate.

Why are you supporting SUMI? He asked

"My father studied there," She replied.

"But you should be supporting me?" He said casually.

"*Issss*! No way! She said with what in Nepali is called *Loparnu,* which means to quickly draw down the curved fingers from forehead to chin with the palm facing the other's face, marking vehement disagreement. She stressed further, "I will support him, no matter what," The crowd buzzed again, some in excitement and some in agony.

They came out of the restaurant and decided to be together till the match got over. As they were chatting in one of the corners in the bus stand, a beggar came begging. To ensure her catch from them, the beggar said, "Please give, I will pray you shall get married." Hari quietly smiled and he could see Kavita chuckling. He thought of giving ten rupees but handed a twenty rupee note instead. The nerve wracking encounter was finally over and Kumudini Homes had dethroned the reigning champions. It was not safe to hang around anymore. Hari reckoned that they leave for home.

> *The best and most beautiful things in the world*
> *cannot be seen or even touched…they must*
> *be felt with the heart – Helen Keller*

Chapter XI

Detached

We often fail to realize the pace of Time. It was not an exception for the two love birds.

Three years passed by and it was time for them to leave Siliguri. Kavita's father would come the next day to take her home. So for the last night they planned to stay together. It was the 17 June 2006. The love birds were aware that it was the last night together in their nest. The night was marked with profound sadness and the feeling of unknown anticipation. The hitherto joy of togetherness had somehow recoiled in oblivion. Hari volunteered to prepare dinner that night and it would of course be a special one. Later each and every moment spent together would pile up in their neatly arranged romantic rack of thoughts. They talked about their future, how often they would meet. Especially meeting would be difficult. They embraced each other and Kavita broke into tears.

Seeing her in tears Hari controlled his own and restraining the unexplained pain, he said, "Please don't cry dear, we will always be in touch okay!" His eyes were moist and his heart, heavy. "And know that I really love you a lot," He tightened his embrace as he uttered these lines. At the backdrop a song was playing soft.

"All my bags are packed I am ready to go, I am standing here outside your door, I hate to wake you up to say good bye…"

With her every sob, her grasp would tense up a bit making him feel all the more void. In sometime, Kavita released herself from his arms and went to a drawer. She came with a paper-wrapped packet and gave it to Hari.

"Open it only when I am gone," Said she.

"But why?"

"No arguments… just promise."

"Promise"

That night they slept in each other's arms, loving more passionately as if the world would crash anytime. How difficult it is to meet and more difficult to part with the one whom you want to spend your life with. Next day they woke up at eight in the morning. He left for his room immediately. Kavita's father could arrive anytime.

He silently sat on his couch in a despondent mood. I could sense his intense contemplation so chose not to disturb him. All those three years he had hardly stayed apart from her. It was only during vacations that they went home. But they were always the last to leave and first to arrive. He didn't know what to do. At that very moment his phone rang, he got up, informed me and left for her room. I told him that we would all be there soon to see her off.

He was going to meet a man about whom he had heard of so often. In her priority list it was her father who ranked number one. He knew how much she loved her father and how would he never decline any wish of hers. Hari knew well that if he was unable to impress him, she would never be his, as simple and as serious as that.

Mr. Giri was a man in his early sixties had a medium height with a clear face and a small moustache; bearing a faint resemblance to his daughter. He was a proud retired government official who had worked very hard all his life to ensure a comfortable life for his family. His two daughters were his most precious jewels. He had in fact declined many transfers and promotions just to be with his family.

"Papa, meet my friend Hari of whom I used to talk to you about," She said as she introduced him.

Hari greeted him with a ready '*Namaste*'.

His scanning eyes perhaps had already given him the necessary report. By now he must have known that the guy in front of him is his adversary. After all who can befool parents? They seem to know it all. He seemed not very keen on warming up.

The owner arrived just then to settle all pending bills and with it the brewing tension relieved a bit. Another tension that now grew within Hari was about the owner mentioning their secret to Kavita's father. Thankfully he did not.

All of us headed towards Kavita's room and she introduced us to her father. We had a formal chat with him though he spoke much less than we would have liked.

Kavita turned towards Hari and wanting to seem casual, said, "Hari can you come with me to the market? You see I have to buy a few things and you know the places better than me. I mean if you are free."

"I am absolutely free," Replied Hari in a haste. Mr. Giri wanted to object but since it was his daughter's choice, he refrained. However, he said, "I too have to buy some fruits; I think I should also come along."

"No papa you are tired. You stay. Don't worry, I will get the fruits. You see after the night's rain it's really hot and humid outside."

He simply nodded and proclaimed "Come back soon or else we will be late."

They went and we chose to help her father in packing the remaining stuff and loading it in the cab.

So they were together again in a rickshaw, may be for the last time holding hands. So many times in the past they had gone together this way, but today it was different. They didn't know where fate would lead them. He kept holding her hands and at times hugged her impervious to what the others would think. He realized that it was just a matter of few hours now, he could neither hold her back, nor freeze the moment.

Normally her shopping would last for hours but it was very quick that day. He never complained about her long shopping hours but today he cursed the pace with which it ended.

Time passes so quickly that we often forget to tell people how much we care and how much they mean to us. On their way back silently cuddled up together in the rickshaw, he wondered if he had loved her enough and cared for her as much, when he had time. Hari however, felt satisfied thinking that whatever he had done for Kavita was honest and full of love. But all that awaited him now was an abyss of loneliness.

All her bags had been packed by now and we had finished transporting the luggage from the room to the cab. Soon it was time for the most painful moment, the moment to part.

Hari wished Kavita a bon voyage but she said nothing; she just nodded. She didn't even look at him. The engine started and so raced his heart, in fact theirs. She was gone, he kept waving his hands but she didn't even turn to look at him. The car gradually receded into distance.

Soon after, a message beeped in his mobile,

"Sorry I didn't even look at you. I didn't want to cry in front of my father. Thank you for everything that you have done and given me; loads of love. And do take lots of care and do have your food on time."

He felt heavy and exhaled a melancholic breath. Another message beeped, "By the way I have left a few things for you apart from the things I gave you last night. Get it from your closet." He wondered how she had managed to do that. He didn't crack his head for the answer though.

For Hari, time seemed to have come to a halt and every minute seemed a lifetime from the moment she had left. He was frantic, didn't know what to do. He took a *prolonged* bath.

Meanwhile we decided to play cards; the loser would have to prepare the evening tea. We decided on most of the chores that way. We asked Hari to join us but he declined. He instead went to the room and opened his closet. It was a huge packet of novels bearing a note that read, "I know it will be hard for you to pass your time without me. So I want you to read all these books, however boring you may find them.

P.S. I want to hear you relate all these stories to me when we meet next. And believe me it's not that far. Now can I get that beautiful smile of yours?"

He opened the other packet which she had given to him the previous night. It contained a pen, a pen holder and a diary gracefully concealing yet another note which said, "I want you to write down your feelings in the diary. Whatever you feel just write, maybe it's about something which may not be related to me, anything, but do also write about how you feel, what you do and how much you miss me. I will read it the next time we meet. And I want you to keep that pen holder in front of you always. I know I don't need a penholder to make myself reminded; I am deep down inside your heart, safe and secure. But do keep it in front of you." He placed the penholder on his table and there it was engraved with a marker pen in her hand writing,

"UR IMPERFECTIONS ARE WHAT MAKE U BEAUTIFUL."

He continued reading, "Yes your imperfections are what make you beautiful. When I met you, you didn't even know how to make fluent conversations. I must tell you, you were damn boring. Remember when we used to go to restaurants, you were not aware of many dishes and I had to literally explain them to you. You always feared the crowd and were so ignorant of so many things. I never had met one with such imperfections. Your dressing sense was really un-understandable and your taste of music was hopeless. In fact, there are so many instances of imperfections that I can find no words to depict. But then it is those gracious imperfections of yours that make you insanely sweet and absurdly beautiful or absurdly sweet and insanely beautiful, whatever way you take."

That night he poured his loneliness and wrote, "Today I have understood more about the love between us. This distance, though not so far, has given me a terrible pain and I guess it's the same with you. I am feeling like a body without its soul, roaming everywhere without any destiny, and I see you everywhere and thus am intensely missing you. I miss your bright shiny eyes, your soft lips and gentle touch. In fact, I miss the whole lot of you. When we meet next time, I want to tell you that I have understood that I cannot live without you, not even a single day. And I shall not let you go away. But till that glorious time arrives, I shall wait." Tears dribbled down his cheeks. Little later he browsed the books given by her. The first one he read was 'The Monk Who Sold His Ferrari'.

Only in the agony of parting do we look into
the depths of love – George Eliot

Chapter XII

A Brisk Meet

Four months passed by and they met only once during that time. It was then she told him about the plans her parents had for her.

Kavita's cousin was in an influential post in one of the agencies of the United Nations and wanted her to visit him so that he would be able to get her a job. Her other cousin in Dubai too wanted Kavita to come with her. Her future was open and secure but she just didn't want to part from Hari. She made excuses and especially convinced her parents that she would search for a job either in Darjeeling or Siliguri. Probably her parents, by now, knew very well why suddenly Siliguri had become so important to her. She would get the inkling of it through their puns.

However, there was one important thing which she had told him in that brisk meeting.

"My parents, I think they don't like you. They want me to get married to an army captain who is the son of my father's friend. So you better get a job soon or else it will be difficult for me."

Hari had replied, "But you know I want to work for the needy. I want to acquire decent qualifications and reach to a level where I can make a difference. And for that I need some time."

It was difficult for them to meet hiding and it was more suffocating to stay away from each other for a longer period of time. Just imagine a fish that comes out of the water accidentally, or a bird that falls on the ground on being hit by a catapult. Their suffocation was such. A life they lived but not wholeheartedly. After all how is it possible to live incomplete? Together they were complete, together they were life.

Whenever they met, time seemed to be moving like a bullet and the same cruel time seemed to move slower than a snail when they were apart, adding more pain to their agony. She would create reasons to visit Siliguri but wouldn't always be able to convince her parents. The adversity was such that neither of them knew 'What next?' Nevertheless they were in constant search for occasions and a little outlet for their togetherness.

Love has a way of making us feel a pain that somehow lingers on. A distance that keeps widening and all we can do is keep believing that something better is coming.

Chapter XIII

Weird Plan

Finally the day came when they took a major decision, crossed all limits, lost their sanity and proved their love for each other. Proved that all they wanted was to be with each other and nothing else. They both desirably devised a plan. She convinced her parents that she would search for a job in Siliguri within a month's time, if not she would go to either of her cousins and try her hand out there. Hari had already arranged a room for her. Soon they were back to the same old golden times doing the things they used to. By now one of Hari's cousin sister Deepa who was in Siliguri had come to know about his love affair. In fact Deepa and Kavita had now become good friends.

Life was great and both of them were so engrossed in each other. More than a fortnight had already gone by and she was now left with little over a week's time to find a job. It was near to impossible. Just two days were left and the situation was no different. It was time either to part or to do something out of the box.

Hari was tensed and as always sought my advice. We decided to consult with our roommates. Friend in need is a friend indeed! And the help came in the form of a weird plan. It was unanimously decided that the only way out was a 'holy lie'.

Kavita would lie to her parents that she had got a job. In a way it was easy because she didn't have to send money to her parents. It was also difficult as they wouldn't have much money at their disposal. Hari used to get Rs. 3500 per month as pocket money out of which Rs. 1800 was by default allotted for food and the rent. All he had was Rs.1700 for everything else. However it was not a petty amount back then when a beer would cost just a forty bucks.

According to the plan Kavita was to stay at Deepa's house. Thankfully she happily accepted to help. Since they were fond of Hari, her in-laws did not object to Kavita's lodging with them. However, another problem was that Deepa's house was quite far, which meant Hari would have to walk all the way or take a rickshaw every day. Either of the prospects seemed bleak to him. The problem was however solved when Hari's friend Saurav offered to lend his bicycle on a condition that it should be at the owner's disposal in situations of emergency. But a problem still persisted. Hari didn't know how to ride a bicycle and he decided to learn from the very next day. Meanwhile Kavita was to go back home for a week and come with her complete set of belongings.

Hari dedicatedly set himself to learn cycling and soon it was time for him to venture out on his first double ride.

The whole week he had sweated a lot and now was ready to test his caliber in the enigmatic gullies where cars, bikes, or rather everything moveable would appear without any signal. He normally felt confident; even if he would fall or get hit by another bicycle or anything, he would simply get up, dust himself off and ride again. But today it was 'her' in the pillion and it unnerved him. What if she fell and hurt herself? – The thought plagued him. He almost hit everything that came on the way but fell down only once— quite a feat for the first-timer.

> *The measure of who we are is what we do*
> *with what we have – Vince Lombardi*

Chapter XIV

Brown Spotted Moral Science

Love was in the air, but in reality times were difficult. Kavita understood the predicament and suppressed all her desires, a great sacrifice indeed! She was a shopaholic and savings was not her cup of tea. They would meet often and at times would go to the market. How Hari wished he could take her to fancy restaurants but all he could afford was small wayside *dhabas*. Hari would at times ask for some extra money from home and buying of books being the most repeated of excuses. They lived under such 'desired undesirability' for three long months. In fact, it was an eventful experience, rather a practical one amidst the utopia of love.

Kavita made it a point to browse for job ads everyday in newspapers. Both realized that perhaps, Eagles had got it wrong when they sang 'Love will keep us alive'.

It was the month of January and Kavita's birthday was approaching. This made Hari feel bad as he wouldn't have enough money to plan an elaborate birthday celebration. He made a phone call to his dad telling him that he needed to buy books.

The voice on the other end said, "By now you must have built a library, son!"

Hari didn't ask for it again.

Kavita tried to comfort him by saying that the greatest gift for her would be to spend the whole day with him. He wanted to ask his friends for help but his insanely absurd philosophies did not allow him to do so. He thought it better not to gift her anything with the borrowed money as it was her birthday and not an ordinary occasion.

*

18 February, her birthday, Hari got up early in the morning, took a shower and went to the temple nearby. He then went to *Court More*, bought a rose and rushed towards his sister's place. Thanks to reckless cycling coupled with almost empty streets he reached there in no time. Kavita was sleeping then. He tiptoed into her room and woke her up with a kiss on the forehead and wished her, "Happy birthday," He gave her the rose.

That day he had some Rs.1200 with him. Hari expressed his desire to take her out for lunch.

They were going to the market after a long time and Kavita was busy window shopping. Hari felt bad then and said, "Dear, I am so sorry. Probably if you were at home you would have had a grand time."

"Shut up, do you intend to fight even today? I am really enjoying my time with you," said Kavita.

She continued, "Past few months have been difficult for both of us financially, but honestly, I love each and every moment spent with you. I like looking at you every time, everything you do, especially your small things, makes me feel special. Please love me as you have loved me all these years and don't you dare leave me," She wrapped her hand around his as she uttered the last line.

She understood that it was her constant window shopping that made him feel bad so she against her instinct pretended as if nothing in the market interested her anymore.

As they passed by a shop she suddenly saw something that magnetised her into the shop. Hari followed her. She glued herself before a pair of beautiful sandal with brown dots. She enquired for the price.

"baroh shau," the shopkeeper replied.

"Look Hari it's so beautiful, you like it?" She said without a second thought.

She immediately corrected herself by saying, "But the shape isn't great!"

To this the shopkeeper said, "What are you saying, it has a perfect shape," And indeed it had, even Hari knew it.

"Let's go Hari," Asserted Kavita.

"Listen Madame we can negotiate the price, if it's too high. How much will you give?"

"*Bhaiya* twelve hundred is too costly, how about nine hundred," Said Hari in an impulse.

"Please let's go dear, I don't want it," Kavita nudged him and gestured not to negotiate.

"Nine hundred is too less," Said the shopkeeper, and the haggling started.

Hari finally declared, "Nine hundred and fifty is all that I can afford. Please *bhaiya*, it's her birthday, please give it," The shopkeeper seemed fine with the price and Hari took out the 80 percent of the money he had and handed it to the shopkeeper.

There was no boundary to Kavita's happiness but still she whimpered, "Why on earth did you have to do this? Now we won't have any money left."

"Don't think much dear. I know you really liked it and it's your birthday. Don't worry I still have 500 bucks back at my room."

"Promise?" She said.

"Promise," He lied. Commitment and pure affection triumphed over his 'Moral Science'. Sometimes lying does what honesty cannot. The immense joy that he could see in her face made the lie nobler.

"Okay then, thank you so much," She said brimming with joy.

"Guess you are hungry, let's go to the hawkers," They both laughed. They had an egg roll and ten *pani puris* each. They bought some sweets for Deepa and her little daughter. By then he was almost broke. From there, they usually hired a rickshaw to get back but today they would have to walk.

Out of difficulties grow miracles — Jean de la Bruyere

Chapter XV

Stabilizing Times

One morning Hari received a message from Kavita regarding her call for an interview and he was to accompany her. She eventually got selected as a stock accountant in an outlet store and was offered Rs. 15,000 a month.

Their austerity finally got over and they were able to repay their debts in the first month itself. They both decided that Kavita would continue to stay at his sister's place or else it would seem ungrateful. He also felt secure keeping her with Deepa. Now his duty was to drop her at her workplace in the morning and pick her up in the evening. On weekends, he would also prepare and carry lunch for her and they would have it together. By now Hari had become a decent cook having a great knack for preparing delicious food. He would learn a recipe and would give it his own twist. In fact, he learnt many new dishes just because she liked them. Whenever she said she liked a particular dish, he would learn and lavishly cook it for her. She would be so happy then and that happiness would give him immense pleasure.

Hari would always be there on time and never made her wait. He did everything she asked for. In fact, he did more than what she asked for. Sometimes Kavita had to go for late night parties with her colleagues. Hari didn't like it and so she had curtailed it to the minimum but sometimes she just couldn't avoid and he would understand. He would wait for her no matter how long the party lasted. He would pick her up and drop her home. By then everyone in her workplace had come to know about their affair and many may have envied their relationship. Kavita on her part had moulded herself to his liking in ways more than one. A testimony of it she proved by wearing long t-shirts as he didn't like her wearing tight and teeny ones. He was a bit old fashioned and would prefer Kavita wearing *kurta pyjamas* which she did quite often though she felt a bit uneasy in them. Her hair had gained a conspicuous length now, it almost touched her hips, and the rollers she often used gave her a gracious look.

People say that love demands the acceptance of the person the way he/she is. However, it's also true that certain compromises should be made giving way to happiness to one's lover. Its best when such things are done without coercion. Hari never forced her to his ways. She did it at her will, just to see the happiness in Hari's face and that was the perfect part of it.

What she didn't change was her shopping spree. She wasted considerable amount of her salary in buying clothes and other things. But whenever she bought anything for herself, she did not forget to buy him something. He would feel awkward taking so many gifts but had no option but to accept. She would flood him with gifts mostly clothes. It was amazing; she knew exactly what he wanted and what suited him the best. She would buy his favorite edibles; most of which were relished by us instead. She really loved him a lot. I am not trying to equate her love with material objects, but the fact that she took care of every little thing related to Hari was indeed remarkable. Most importantly, she must be credited for improving Hari's dressing sense; good enough to turn a few heads.

With each passing day their relationship grew stronger and stronger. In fact, it was like wine getting better with time. They had not only immense love between them but also a great deal of understanding and respect for each other. Like in most of the cases wherein complacency creeps into relationships after a couple of years or so; theirs was different. Hari loved, cared and respected her as always. More importantly, he had kept the romanticism alive.

Don't judge each day by the harvest you reap but by the seeds that you plant – Robert Louis Stevenson

Chapter XVI

Nurse and the Brandy Lullaby

It was one of those summers that Hari's sister and her family had gone for a vacation to Shimla, a hill station in India. Meanwhile, Kavita had seriously fallen ill. It initially started with fever and then transcended into vomiting. He at once took her to the doctor. She was feeling very weak and Hari stood holding her all the time, praying for her progress.

The doctor finally arrived and ordered his assistant to open the chamber. Kavita was the first one to be examined. Hari had already secured the appointment. She was to go alone. The doctor after her check-up asked about the escort who had come with her.

"A friend," was all what Kavita told the doctor.

"I did notice you two at the reception and it seems your friend really cares about you," The doctor had said directing Hari to come inside.

Hari immediately asked, "What is the problem with her Doctor?"

"Apparently it looks like viral infection, just undergo the prescribed tests," He said handing him the prescription.

The doctor further advised, "And yes, she has to get admitted for a complete check up," Kavita turned towards Hari and gave him a sullen look.

Hari described his predicament to the doctor, and reckoned, "Doctor I will give her the medicines on time and will take utmost care but please don't admit her."

"Son, it can't be that way. She needs to be admitted," The doctor could discern the disappointment on his face so he said, "Do one thing; admit her for now, if she gets better by five in the evening you can take her home and if not you are left with no choice."

He added, "By five the reports will be out, and if she is fine I will discharge her."

Probably this was for the first time the doctor had given such leverage. He smiled and patted Hari as he left. Kavita was given a bed after she had undergone a few tests. Hari sat near her holding hands and hugging her at times only to make the co-patients stare.

"Dear how are you feeling now?" Hari asked after sometime.

"Bit better," She concluded. Perhaps it was a bit of psychology that was working rather than the medicine.

After a while Hari said, "I think you should take some rest, meanwhile I will go, clean up the house and prepare lunch for us."

Kavita would not agree to this. Hari massaged her head and let her sleep and when he was convinced she had slept, he slowly disengaged himself from her and went out to fulfill the errands he needed to. Before leaving he asked the patients around to inform her that he would be back soon. He didn't have much time so he hired an auto rickshaw. He hurriedly cleaned the room, the kitchen, washed the previous day's utensils, boiled water, cooked some plain food for her, packed it in a hot case and was on his way to the hospital on his darling cycle. On the way, he bought some fruits and a packet of her favorite chips. He looked at his watch; all these had taken him a mere one and a half hours. He came back at a blistering pace. Kavita was already awake by the time he reached there. She at once cuddled up to him like a child.

"I missed you, so bad of you to leave me alone," She complained.

"Sorry, I had to go but see what I have brought for you."

She was about to open the packet of chips when he snatched it saying, "Only after lunch and medicines."

The doctor came for the afternoon visit. "How are you feeling young lady?" He inquired. And with a smile he added, "Is your friend taking care of you?"

"Yes I am feeling better. Can I go home doctor?"

"No, not yet; only after I see the report in the evening. If things are normal you can leave."

After examining the report in the evening, the doctor called Hari and said, "The report is not that alarming, it's probably her stress at work that has put her to this, but I advise you to admit her for at least a day or two. Just to be sure," He added, "Now it's up to you to decide."

"Doctor I would like to take her home and I will take proper care of her," He asserted in one go.

"I know you will but what if something goes wrong, what will you do?"

"I will handle it don't worry," He said with confidence.

"Okay, then take her at your own risk."

Hari was about to leave when the Doctor asked him to wait. He handing out his visiting card said, "If there's any problem, call me up." Hari was surprised by such a gesture from the doctor but thanked him warmly.

*

Two days had passed but the medication was not doing much good. He informed me about the situation and sought my advice. I thought her sickness had prolonged because of her sleeplessness. So I told him, "Hari whatever I tell you now may seem ridiculous but just try it once, it will help her." I gave him the direction to which he hesitantly agreed.

"Won't there be any negative reaction?" He asked.

"No just try it," I assured.

So he gave it in a glass and asked her to gulp it down. At first she didn't agree to try the remedy but gave in finally after much pampering.

What was the remedy? A peg of brandy!

After a while it started to have its effect and she started feeling dizzy. To a novice one glass does wonders. And that's precisely what happened with her. Hari would tell me later how she started behaving strangely. She became sweetly garrulous after a few minutes. She asked him to hug her and tell her how much he loved her. He found no apt words and said metaphorically the commonly uttered lines, "Deeper than the ocean and as vast as the sky," She gave an intoxicated smile.

"Listen I am drunk but please don't tell this to anyone. Sshhhh…. speak slowly otherwise the neighbors will know that I am drunk," She whispered into his ears.

When he told me about this the next day, I could feel that the episode must have been sweet and hilarious as he bore a perpetual smile throughout his narration. I presumed that the memory of the incident would make him smile whenever he recounted it.

The absurdity had actually proved to be an effective remedy. He would constantly wake up to see if she was awake, but she was not. She finally had slept soundly after five days. This also meant he too hadn't slept for same number of days. In fact, he had slept much less as he would constantly get up to check on her. He had situated his bed on the floor so as not to disturb her. He took utmost care of her and didn't go for his classes even. The whole day he would be with her, taking care of her, cooking her bland food, feeding her, giving her medicines on time. She was a cleanliness freak so he made it a point to keep the house and especially her room neat and tidy.

In this nursing endeavor his own health had deteriorated. It seemed as if he was the one sick and under medication.

> *Grow old along with me! The best is*
> *yet to be – Robert Browning*

Chapter XVII

Prashant Phenomenon and the Aftermath

Life was on the roll. Meanwhile Prashant, a local lad, from Darjeeling had made the hills proud by reaching to the top ten in the television singing reality show, Indian Idol. After months of tussle Prashant had been crowned the Indian Idol. A tremendous feat for a Nepali to be at the helm of the country whose victory was being seen as the victory of the whole Nepali community. Although Amit, his fellow contestant was a much better singer, it was the *voting* support of the Nepalis all across the country and the globe that helped him win.

While there was an ambience of gaiety and merriment, a derogative comment as, *"Nepali ko Indian Idol bana diya ab hamara ghar, mohallae ki chowkidari kaun karega?"*, meaning "now that a Nepali has been made an Indian Idol, who will guard our homes and our locality?" by a radio Jockey of 93.5 Red FM came as a hard blow to the Nepalis everywhere. Silent procession was taken out on 28th September as a mark of protest against the scathing statement.

We decided to take part in the rally too. As we approached the *Court More* junction the procession was provoked and a communal riot broke out. We ran into opposite directions; Sudhan, Millen and I hurriedly entered into one of the government buildings.

"Where are the others?" Sudhan shouted in frenzy. The Bengalis were taking the Nepalese out and beating them mercilessly; even the women folk were not spared! We were petrified.

Sudhan called up Sashil and I called Hari.

"Where are you?" I asked him.

"I am in one of the buildings near *Dinabandhu Manch*," Said Hari.

I shouted back, "Who is with you?"

Hari cried from the other end, "Wangdi and some other Nepalis."

"And what about others?" I cried.

"I don't know," He shouted.

Meanwhile Sudhan was talking to Sashil. We felt a bit relieved to know that the others were with him. The situation was still volatile.

We remained there for many hours huddled up against each other. There was a boy next to us. And Millen happened to ask, "*Som chai kaha ko?*" *Som* is a synonym to 'mate' in

Australia, very commonly used in Darjeeling by male folks to designate a friend or a comrade.

"I am a Manipuri," The boy replied.

"Were you there in the rally too?" asked Sudhan.

"No I live in *Pradhan Nagar* and had come here for some errand."

"So they chased you thinking that you are a Nepali," I commented.

He gave a forlorn smile.

As we were communicating with others to regroup and go back to our room, the Manipuri boy said, "Can I come with you? At this point of time I can't return to my room."

"Yah, sure why not, please come," Said Sudhan.

Finally we returned to the room around midnight. On the way Millen said, "There may be some groups patrolling at the moment. Guys if we happen to meet any such groups; we will go down fighting. And nobody will run; we will fight till we can. Clear?" We all nodded including the Manipuri and Hari.

Thankfully we reached our room safe and sound and our conversation started.

Sudhan said, "These guys contend that Darjeeling is a part of West Bengal, but see how they treat us."

"And Prashant, serves in Kolkata Police," Mingma added.

"Probably it's just Darjeeling not its people that is its part," Said Wangdi.

"This is the reason why we need Gorkhaland," I proclaimed.

"Gorkhaland?" asked the Manipuri.

"You don't know? But many in the Northeast are aware of it."

"Sorry I am not," Said the Manipuri.

I continued, "See friend, Gorkhaland Movement basically refers to the age old demand of the Gorkhas for a separate state of their own within the Indian union. The movement actually aims to distinguish Indian Nepalese from the nationals of Nepal."

Wangdi added, "This precisely is the reason as to why the Indian Nepalese prefer to call themselves Gorkhas and their language Gorkhali rather than Nepali. However, when the Eighth Schedule of the constitution was amended in 1992 to make it a scheduled language, the term Nepali instead of Gorkhali was listed."

Sashil chose to elaborate it further, "There are grave misconceptions about our Indian identity as we are easily confused as citizens of Nepal. Hence, the movement can be seen as a fervent plea, not to tag the Nepalis of India as foreigners."

Wangdi elaborated, "The demand for Gorkhaland is actually not only driven by the identity crisis but also a question of self determination and about participation of the Gorkhas in the Indian national governance, thereby accelerating their integration in the national mainstream. Moreover, it is also a demand to reclaim the lost territory."

"Lost territory?" The Manipuri seemed confused.

I added, "In fact, Darjeeling and its adjoining areas were never parts of West Bengal prior to 1866. The history of Darjeeling runs closely with Nepal, Bhutan and Sikkim. Darjeeling District including Kalimpong, a subdivision of present Darjeeling was part of Western Sikkim. After Prithvi Narayan Shah, the great Nepali imperialist's conquest and unification of greater Nepal, Darjeeling came to be a part of Nepal."

"What happened next?" He fuelled his curiosity.

I replied back, "The disagreement over the frontier policy of the Gorkhas resulted in a war in 1814 by the British and by the treaty of Saghawlee in 1815, the Nepalese ceded 7000 square miles of territory to the British. Only a part of the region ceded from Nepal was returned to Sikkim by the Treaty of Titalia in 1817. But it was taken back again by the British for the purpose to build a sanitarium in 1835. The remaining parts of Darjeeling and its adjoining areas were taken by the British by means of annexation. In 1706, Kalimpong was taken by Bhutan from the rajah of Sikkim which it retained till 1865. Under the Treaty of Sinchula between Bhutan and the East India Company in 1865, a part of Dooars and Kalimpong were ceded to the Company."

The young man from Manipur exclaimed "O... you seem to know a lot!"

Sashil immediately added, "You know my friend, what the irony is? Most of our people even our politicians are not in the knowhow of the core issues related to history, politics and identity. But yes the consciousness among the Gorkha youths is gradually building up."

"Right! you are, absolutely right. I can sense that," Said the Manipuri and shook his hands with all and said, "I am Sanayaima from Ukhrul district of Manipur. It's an honour to meet you all."

We shook hands with him and the introduction followed.

Sanayaima said, "Manipur also has problems facing ethnicity," "And you already know the plight of the North-Easterners in main stream India," He added.

He further asked, "Tell me something, what happened to Darjeeling hills after the Treaty of Sinchula?"

I answered back, "During the late 1860s, all these areas were incorporated and kept under Bengal administration for administrative convenience. This particular fact can also be substantiated by the document which was issued by the Government of West Bengal on 29th October 1986 entitled 'Gorkhaland Agitation, The Issues and Information Document' in which it states – "historically what is known as the district of Darjeeling today, was parts of two kingdoms during pre-British period—the kingdoms of Sikkim and Bhutan. Following wars and treaties signed with these two kingdoms, this territory came under the control of British Empire in India."

Millen changed the topic of conversation and said, "This FM jockey should be hacked to death. How dare he call us *chawkidar*?"

"But most of the Indians think so, should they all be hacked too?" said Bristrit.

"We need to change perceptions," Hari spoke for the first time.

"But how? It's easier said than done," Mingma commented.

"These Bengalis I feel like killing them all," Sudhan said in rage.

"Don't say like that," asserted Hari, "I have many good Bengali friends. We have good and bad people anywhere and everywhere; it's just about finding the right ones."

"Yah, that's right. There are many Bengalis who are sympathetic towards your demand," said Bristrit.

"What are you saying? What do you mean by your demand?" asked Sudhan.

"I mean, we from Sikkim have a state of our own and you all deserve one too. We support your demand but it's you who need to fight for it."

Sudhan rudely lashed out, "Imagine one Gorkha telling another Gorkha that Gorkhaland is your demand, how pathetic! Gorkhaland will bring identity to all Gorkhas spread throughout the country."

"There are many Nepalese in Manipur and other Northeastern states so Gorkhaland will definitely bring cheer to all the Gorkhas around," Remarked Sanayaima trying to ease the tension.

"In that case why did Ghishing accept the DGHC in 1986? It was a developmental agency and in doing so it negated the efforts of numerous Gorkhas outside Darjeeling who had fought and lost their lives. Did they fight for the material development of Darjeeling?" asked Bristrit once again.

"And don't forget *our* Sikkim gave refuge to *your* people during the Gorkhaland Movement of 1986," Bristrit continued.

"Thank you for giving us refuge, then," Sudhan punned and continued, "You being educated don't understand and still think you are a part of another state rather than the community."

"Yes I am proud to be a Sikkimese and only after that I am a Gorkha," Bristrit shouted in anger.

"You people hardly harmonize with us," Sudhan asserted.

"As if you people do," replied Bristrit.

Sensing the escalating tension Sanayaima tried to divert the topic, so he asked, "If Darjeeling was once part of Sikkim then why on earth does it not claim its territory back?"

"Because they are afraid," Cried Sudhan. "They think that we will capture all the resources and outplay them in every sphere."

"But Sikkim does not need to be part of Darjeeling which is full of only clever people always eyeing some bounty," Cried Millen, another Sikkimese.

"*Oey* what do you think you are?" shouted Sudhan.

At this moment both became agitated and Sudhan said, "Fight *khelchas?*"

"*Anta k darauchu jasto lagcha kya, khelum, aija,*" Bristrit replied and Millen and Mingma backed him up.

At this point Wangdi became agitated with the two and said, "What a shame! We live in the same room like brothers and suddenly today one is from Sikkim and the other from Darjeeling. And you two fight at a time when we should be united. He must be mocking at us", he said looking at Sanayaima. "Shame on you two. If we don't unite, a time might come when our caste will become more important than our entity," He prophesized.

This is a serious situation but it makes me drive home a few important facets of Nepali language. This language I feel is aggressive in a way, "Fight *khelchas*" Literally means 'let's play fight,' so fighting here is a play. We don't switch off the light, we 'kill it,' so we say, '*Batti maar.*' We don't initiate a talk rather we 'kill the talk,' so we say '*baat maaroom,*' to list a few.

However, the wedge had been created and the issues got compounded so much so that our group was internally bifurcated and each had to decide his camp.

I asked Hari, "Which side you are in?"

"I don't want to take sides."

I had a few things to vent out, but chose to wait for a time more appropriate.

It was already six in the morning and the eight of us smoked one cigarette to the buds. The cigarette secured a temporary *set-up*. It didn't suffice so we emptied the ash-tray and re-ignited the discarded buds, the procedure which we often repeated during our times of austerity.

*

The following day our Bengali landlady advised us not to go out at any cost and if there was anything we needed, we should tell her.

"And don't you all worry," She said, "I will not let anything happen to you all; you are my responsibility now," She emphasized.

We warm heartedly thanked for her concern.

After days of hiding, the army came to our rescue and we were taken to Kalimpong. Meanwhile, Kavita continued staying with Hari's sister as it was basically a Nepali locality and thus was safe.

Nevertheless the incident had created a deep chasm between the Nepalis and the non-Nepalis.

*

When we came back to Siliguri after a month's sojourn Hari went straight to Kavita.

It was still not safe even after months of the *Court More* incident but Hari always went to drop and pick her up as usual. I was worried for him and would tell him, "I think you shouldn't go to receive her. Her workplace is near your sister's house so she can manage it, come on! Don't risk your life like this."

"No man I can't dare to do that, if something happens to her I will not be able to bear it nor forgive myself."

"But what about you?" I asked.

"I'll manage, don't worry," Said Hari.

Life went on as it was before.

What lies behind you and what lies in front of you, pales in comparison to what lies inside you – Ralph Waldo Emerson

Chapter XVIII

And So it Happened

Kavita's parents were now worried about her safety. Moreover, the incident gave them the right opportunity to take her away from Siliguri. They immediately applied for Kavita's visa.

Her father came to meet her. By now her family and Deepa were in constant touch, they are, I guess till date. But what they were unaware was that she was Hari's sister. During his two days' stay he made it absolutely clear that she would have to quit her job within a month's time.

Now there was no way they could carry on. Hari too had thought deep and finally gave in, he would let her go. One fine evening he told her,

"Listen dear I think you should go now. Even I will be completing my Masters and will have to move somewhere for further studies."

"So now you want me to go since you can pursue your career the way you want? Remember if I had thought about my career too, I would have been long gone," She nitpicked.

"No! You don't get it, what I mean is, we will build our careers within the next five years and get married. And don't you think we need to get serious now? In fact, I am not happy with the job you are in, you definitely deserve a better one and I am also worried about your safety," Said Hari.

The very next week she submitted her resignation but had to serve a month's notice according to the corporate contract. In the meantime, Kavita opened a *Facebook* account on his behalf which could possibly be a vital link when she would be away. That month they spent most of their times together. Finally the time had arrived for them to part their ways. And so it happened.

Why can't we get all the people together in the world that we really like and then just stay together? I guess that wouldn't work. Someone would leave. Someone always leaves. Then we would have to say good-bye. I hate good-byes. I know what I need. I need more hellos – Charles M. Schulz

Chapter XIX

Communication Dent

Within weeks of her return to home, things began to change. Kavita could not devote much time there on. Family was a priority now. Hari, on the other hand would constantly fiddle with his phone waiting for that *antidote* call.

It so happened one evening, Kavita lost in her only conversation of the day failed to avoid her father's confrontation.

"I have been noticing you since a few days now. You seem to be on the phone all the time. What's the matter?" He asked.

Since then even their night calls reduced alarmingly. The communication gap which had plagued their relation years back marked its advent yet again.

One day Kavita told Hari that she would not be able to talk to him for a week as she would be visiting her relatives in some remote village *still* devoid of *Edison's touch*. Nothing of this sort had ever happened in their long courtship. He missed her a lot and his continuous dialing of her phone number simply went futile.

*

After a week she called him up.

"My god how are you, you know I missed you so much. So how was your stay?" He said in one go.

"Actually I have to tell you one thing, I didn't go at all," Said Kavita.

"What! Where were you then?" He asked.

"I was at home," Came her cold reply.

"So why on earth, didn't you call me and why was your phone switched off, this is not done, seriously not done," Yelled Hari and disconnected the phone. He felt raged after so many years. I mean I have known him for long but never had I seen him so angry. She called him incessantly but he did not answer her calls.

She messaged him saying, "Hey dear I am extremely sorry. Actually I am passing through a difficult phase of my life, don't know what to do. I am so confused and feeling so lonely. So lied to you to take time for myself and decide on things. Please forgive me, just once."

Hari immediately melted and called her up, "Please don't do this ever again; you don't know how lonely I feel without you and by the way what's bothering you so much?"

"No, it's just a family matter and it has almost been solved," She professed.

Her family matters were not unknown to him. This must be a far more serious matter he reckoned. But he could not fathom what her words or her gestures could possibly mean.

The dent in communication was a perceived threat constantly looming large. Hari could sense his sky changing colours.

Even if they managed to speak over the phone, it would be cold with nothing much to say. This would frustrate Hari and would lead to quarrels between the two. Hari to cheer her up would talk about the past; about the things he had done which she had told him to do; the new recipes he had learnt for her and so on. But nothing was working. Indeed the problem seemed alarmingly serious.

Meanwhile our final exams got over and we decided to leave the next day. However, some would return later to join a coaching institute for civil services exam, another glaring trend among the Gorkha youths. Hari, who was a batch junior to us had his exams later so he had no choice but to stay back alone.

Hope is the power of being cheerful in circumstances
that we know to be desperate – G.K. Chesterton

Chapter XX

The Improbable

It was eight in the morning when Hari was woken up by a message beep. It was one of his school friends Sagar who had sent him a forwarded message proclaiming that the particular day was something special and if one wished for anything it would come true. These kinds of messages are always on the run. He ignored the message and didn't wish for anything. He had it all, a good family, a desired career that he was building, great bunch of friends, and to ice it up, Kavita. He got up and started to clean his room.

As he was cleaning, his phone rang and at once he knew it was Kavita, owing to the ring tone he had assigned.

"I am sorry," She said with a sobbing voice.

"Why are you saying sorry and please don't cry."

But she kept on pleading for forgiveness and with every sorry, her sobs only got heavier.

"Please, tell me what has happened?" He said frantically.

After moments of silence she finally revealed… "I am engaged."

The words hit him with all its might. His blood froze. He thought of too many things at the same time. He was in a state of trance. Every moment he had spent with her came as a flashback. Whatever she had just revealed reverberated in his ears until he felt the salty warmth of much preserved emotions rolling down his face.

All he could say was, "If that's what makes you happy, it's ok."

He wanted to say so many things but words just would get strangled inside his throat. He found himself in an emotional dungeon. He threw the phone on his bed without disconnecting it and lurched towards the corner of his room. He sat there heavily, covered his face and cried till he could cry no more.

I was the first one he shared the news with. His voice faltered as he gave me the news. I was very confused and couldn't take it. They were perfect and I had assumed their love story would have a fairy tale ending. But fate always has an upper hand. It gives a twist at the very last moment, changing lives drastically, sometimes for good and most of the times for bad. This particular twist had turned his life upside down.

"How could she do this to you? She must have been under some kind of pressure from her parents," I uttered with desperation.

"If you want I can talk to her parents," I added.

I thought after all they did have inkling about their affair. But he just wouldn't let me do it. I enquired about the man with whom she was engaged.

Hari said that Kavita had told him about this man before and used to casually declare that he had an adversary. Hari described his adversary as Kavita's mother's favorite character and her mother always pestered her to marry him. The man was a captain in the army and had enchanted the family with his demeanor which I thought was too perfect to be natural.

"He must be a good guy and I am sure Kavita will be happy with him," He cried as he said this unable to control the spur of emotions.

I felt Kavita's fiancé, the Captain, and Hari were stark contraries. On one side was this most perfect dude with a glorious job filled with valor and on the other side was Hari with his innocent imperfections and a broken heart infused with overflowing love for her. Then I had a feeling that perfection had won its battle over imperfection. Probably his imperfections could not make him beautiful anymore.

His life was in complete disarray. He was not at all prepared for such an eventuality. It was difficult for him especially in the university where he had to pretend to be normal and wear a fake smile on his face.

I had never imagined that such a day would ever come and now that it had, it had changed his life completely. Hari was in a pathetic condition. He resorted to excessive drinking. Next thirteen days, he would tell me much later, he just drank, cried in the corner and did nothing. His exams were round the corner, but he was least bothered. What made him worse and what aggravated his pain were her constant calls. He would avoid it many times but at times he would be vulnerable. Kavita seemed to have settled down and would dispassionately advise him to forget her. She could do this so wonderfully as if the past had just been a momentary dream.

*

It was the day of her engagement. He knew it. He imagined her wearing a fancy dress. Her man beside her, exchanging rings. He couldn't control his tears. Those days he didn't have control over anything, it seemed. Days before he had checked her *Facebook* profile; there she was with her fiancé, her arms wrapped around his. He immediately logged out. Few days later Hari, son of Rudra Hari and grandson of Narhari was *unfriended* from Kavita's *Facebook* friends' list forever and he deactivated his account.

Hari drank and drank and puked around his room. He looked at the spoils and his memory flashed back to a certain phase of his life. That day he had stayed with Kavita at his sister's place and it was his niece's birthday party. He drank that day but he only wanted to drink beer that too just a bottle at the most. Kavita too had given him the green signal to drink. But as it happens in such occasions, somebody had mixed his drink and he went totally out. That night he made her laugh with his silly antics. Everyone had gone off to sleep but all he wanted to do was talk.

In between the talks he suddenly felt nauseous and immediately rushed towards the bathroom. His intoxicated legs couldn't nimble up much pace so he puked on the way. Kavita came rushing behind him. He felt awkward and also bad that he had dirtied the floor, from the kitchen to the bathroom. She gave him a glass of water and helped him to the bathroom asking him to gargle. She washed his face and brought him to a chair. Meanwhile she brought a shabby piece of curtain and started mopping the mess. Seeing this, he felt all the more awkward and had told her,

"Hey I am so sorry, please don't do it, I will clean it up."

"It's ok you be seated."

But today there was no 'she' to clean up his mess. He then imagined her surrounded by her family. All would be dancing around and happy for her.

She had so easily let him out of her life as if he was some unwanted object. He wailed thinking he could never have her in his life again. Her talks, her laughs and her moments would belong to someone else from now.

> *We often get hurt and have to let go the one whom*
> *we want to grow old with, it may be the best thing*
> *that may have happened to you... but this is life... it*
> *goes on... it has to go on... there's no other way*

Chapter XXI

Avenues

Sometimes the only feasible thing to do is to just let it go...

His tears had dried up by the fourteenth day. He got up and cleaned the mess he had created. There were only five days to his exam. It was a 'do or die' situation for it determined his future, his career. He thought about his parents, their sacrifices. He thought about his friends who were extremely worried for him and called him constantly to enquire of his well being.

On that particular day Kavita called him from her new number. He picked the call and she inquired about his whereabouts but he didn't reply. He didn't utter a word and in silence hung up. He immediately typed a message:

"I am your past now, and he is your future. Don't waste your time on me. It is not fair to cheat on him. So please make it your last call if you ever loved me even for a moment. I hope I have made myself clear. Take care and all the best for your future. May god bless you forever!"

He felt heavy as he sent it and heavier as he received the delivery report.

Since that day he had witnessed a strange transformation taking place within him. He was losing his emotions, he felt. He preferred staying alone and most of the calls to him remained unanswered. He was battling against his emotions, against himself, perhaps the toughest battle.

He would evade talking about Kavita to anyone and was reticent about his personal life. Probably he was too distraught to speak about his tragedy. Even if he ever spoke about Kavita, he would always defend her and wouldn't let me or any of his friends rebuke about her, for reasons at least not apparent to me. Strangely though whenever he recounted about her, he just remembered only the good things she had done for him.

Once I had asked him why he used to constantly defend her. He replied, "I can't be ungrateful for so many things she has done for me. You are my friend and you know how much I loved her, but it is me who had received and felt her love and her cares. Just because she is gone doesn't mean that I remember one mistake of hers' and overlook those million times she made me feel special. Though I don't want to see her face and hear her voice ever again, I will never be ungrateful for the good things she has done for me. This is a mistake we all commit. When we are in love we treat them as if there's no one else better. But the moment that person walks out for whatever reasons, we tend to rebuke them. For me that's not right."

Then I couldn't comprehend his cognitive psychology. Now when I think about it, it's probably a way to live. Harbouring of good thoughts fuels our mind with positive vibes while negativity only taints our thinking, demeaning one in turn.

*

After six months results were announced. He was able to secure decent marks but not as good as what he was capable of. But thanks to his previous grades, he was able to secure the much coveted sixty percent which all would aspire and crave for.

That year he went to Calcutta, Lappiere's 'City of Joy'. Joy he got in the city or not, we would discover later but for now he was going to pursue his M.Phil.

It was a new setting and that must have helped him, I thought. But to me he was not the same person. I don't know what had changed in him but he had. When there is an inconspicuous change in the sky, it is only visible to the one who has observed it carefully. Such was the case with my observation of the change in Hari because by now I knew him inside out. I genuinely hoped that this change would be for his own good.

> *Give light, and the darkness will disappear*
> *of itself – Desiderius Erasmus*

Part II

Six months later (2008)

Chapter XXII

Deepening Camaraderie

Life had slowly but steadily returned to some semblance of normality for him. Life in Calcutta, now Kolkata, had geared up pace. M.Phil classes were on in full swing. It was an extremely competitive environment for him where he had to prove his caliber amongst the Bengali intellectuals who were extremely hard working if not more. Shubho and Shambhu became his new close batch-mates. Reema and Swikriti, the two Nepali girls from Sikkim were also in the same batch yet Hari felt awkward to mingle with them.

Reema's dusty wavy hair almost touched her hips and it complemented her fair skin. Her eyes were extremely beautiful and expressive and her lips had a natural pout which was always accentuated by a hint of gloss. Swikriti too had fair skin and bore a very 'girl-next-door' persona. They were both of equal height; not very tall and both dressed quite similarly – t-shirts, jeans and sandals. Swikriti was less communicative while Reema was the extrovert, always chatting with someone or the other in the class.

*

Once on his way back from the university Hari found himself in the same bus boarded by Reema and Swikriti. The two were seated adjacent to him. He greeted them with a smile and plugged his earphone on and started listening to the songs played by the local radio station. He felt a tap on his shoulder as soon as the overcrowded bus disgorged itself at Esplanade, a happening junction. He removed his earphone.

Reema asked, "Where do you stay?"

"I have a rented flat at Manicktala. What about you?"

"We stay in Bhawanipur in a small flat, just the two of us," She replied.

She continued, "Why are you always quiet and do not mingle around?" He just smiled back.

"Would you like to come to our flat?" invited Reema.

"No, thank you. Actually I have some work today and I am already late." He said in circumspection.

"*Jum na hamro room*," She insisted, adding, "Swikriti really makes good coffee and Maggie," to entice him.

He felt it was impolite to deny again so he agreed to go with them.

They got down at Bhawanipur bus stop.

The flat was nice and spacious with two rooms, a kitchen and an attached washroom. It was neat and clean and well arranged, he thought. His was a mess. On the left lay a four-layered bamboo rack. The three layers were stuffed with books in exquisite arrangement. On the topmost shelf *throned* a boastful teddy bear.

Swikriti noticed Hari staring at the teddy and said, "That's Reema's. It was gifted by Aakash, her boyfriend." Reema smiled and quickly added, "And that one is hers, gifted by her boyfriend Sonam," pointing to the right where another teddy lay in identical arrangement.

Swikriti and Reema went to the kitchen giggling. Meanwhile he scanned the books they had. After a while the two entered the room with coffee and egg Maggie. They immediately had struck chords as the girls were cordial and receptive in their approach making Hari's awkwardness vanish in a matter of moments. He found out that Reema's boyfriend was working in a private company as a manager and Swikriti's was working in one of the banks in Kolkata itself. It was obvious that they loved their boyfriends very much, especially Reema.

Swikriti revealed, "You know Hari, Reema and Aakash have a very sweet relation. They are madly in love with each other." Reema blushed and went to the other room saying that she would bring some sweets.

She continued, "Reema constantly tells me that she can't live without him. Sometimes I fear what would happen to her if he ever ditched her."

She quickly added, "But I know he won't, after all he is a very good guy. He treats me like his own sister."

Reema came back with a plate full of *rosogullas*. During the conversation, Hari sub-consciously happened to observe Reema's hair and a thought of Kavita abruptly passed him by. He realized that it would be difficult for him to forget her and wondered if he ever crossed her mind.

Soon it was dark and he had to leave. The evening was remarkable because it marked the beginning of a wonderful friendship between the trio.

After that day the three began having their lunch together. He often went to their room, showed his culinary skills which would mesmerize the girls. He even stayed back when they had plans to booze. The girls would often want to know about his love life but he would evade the matter one way or the other. He couldn't afford to get hurt again. Nevertheless Hari was grateful that he had finally got a company where he felt at home with. In fact, their friendship had blossomed in no time.

*

During vacations they would go together till Siliguri and then part for their respective places. On one such vacation, Reema had invited him to her place. Hari felt very awkward but finally agreed to go with her.

While heading towards Siliguri, a sudden strike had been called by the hill political party and they got stuck at the Coronation Bridge at the National Highway 31. They had *jhaal moori* with raw coconut to pass the time. They also fed the monkeys. Hari asked,

"Do you know where these monkeys came from?"

"Probably from the nearby jungles," Remarked Reema.

"No! They came from our village."

"Don't bluff."

"No! I am serious. Many years ago, our village was troubled by the monkeys. They would destroy our crops, break into our homes and steal food. They even killed many village dogs. So the villagers came up with a plan and laid traps all over the village. Eventually they were all caught except for one. They brought all the monkeys in trucks and *rehabilitated* them here."

"Seriously?" exclaimed Reema and asked, "What happened to the one that didn't fall in the trap?"

"For many days he stayed alone and one day he was found playing with a dog." They both laughed.

The monkeys have, since then become a regular sight at National Highway 31. The sparse forest is inapt for providing them with food so they have resorted to 'begging' I would say. These monkeys thrive on the edibles which some benevolent passengers throw at them. They have forgotten to hunt for food in the forest. I'm afraid a long strike would bring their creed to extinction.

It was during this journey that Hari felt closer to and got more comfortable with Reema. He stayed with her family for two days. When he got back, he was full of praise for their warm hospitality.

He was aware that Reema's parents were quite liberal and had no problems with her having a boyfriend. Yet he had been apprehensive about meeting her parents. But when Reema's father remarked, "I have heard a lot about you from my daughter and wanted to meet you. Now that I have, I am glad." Hari heaved a huge sigh of relief.

However, he couldn't avoid the kitchen as Reema made him the cook there too. He recounted to me how Reema had put him in an awkward position when her parents had offered him a drink. He had declined the offer as he felt discomfited to drink with them. To this she had said,

"In Kolkata you drink gallons, so stop pretending." He looked at her with blank eyes. She just laughed and added, "You can smoke downstairs ok," And there he was, drinking with her parents.

From a small seed a mighty trunk may grow – Aescylus

Chapter XXIII

U Turn

The semester exams were approaching and they got busy with their preparations, and with Hari 'preparation' and 'last moment' went hand in hand. So he was always busy before the exams. Reema and Swikriti suggested that they should study together, as they were also not on their toes. The three would discuss for hours, study individually and discuss again. They would divide the topics to save time and energy. The strategy was a grand success. The exams brought them all the more closer, especially Hari and Reema.

Swikriti most of the times would be over the phone talking to her boyfriend. She often went to his place leaving Reema in the company of Hari. Swikriti's boyfriend, a busy man rarely came to their room.

A week after the exams, it was Reema's third anniversary of her courtship with Aakash. She decided to throw a party. Hari on his part had already composed a message for the two after a considerable amount of thought and time. This was how Hari would make people feel special. He never dared to do big things, he just did small things.

On the anniversary morning, he sent an SMS to Reema, "Happy anniversary. May both of you always find love in each other's heart, may it grow with every fight, every distance, and may your love be strong with each passing day. Pray that you soon be united forever. Once again happy anniversary and please convey my regards to your better half."

Reema replied, "Thank you so much…why don't you wish Aakash urself? He would feel good."

"Ok then forward me his number."

He saved it as Reema's *sky*.

With the passage of time Hari and Reema started talking to each other over the phone quite often; it was Reema who had started the trend. They would talk for long hours about various things ranging from family to friends, to food to love. They in no time realized that they had so much in common.

In fact, Hari felt so comfortable with her that he actually confided about his past life; no one apart from me would ever know about it, at least from Hari. She was amused by his stories and even more by the kind of love he had bestowed on Kavita. He had always held a positive stance about her and would only seek her well-being. This had earned him great respect from Reema, she had told him.

Reema with time also felt at ease sharing things with Hari and she would share all those stuffs which she couldn't share with Aakash or even with Swikriti. Their tete-a-tete spree rocketed all the more. Reema's boyfriend was a busy man.

Moreover, they had already completed three years, drying up all the topics of discussion. Their talk would last for mere five to ten minutes. From her accounts of her boyfriend Hari could discern that he was a very good guy, an understanding person who loved Reema dearly. Sometimes they would fight and it would be due to Aakash's ever so busy schedule. Hari was always there to scold her and would never fail to make her understand things in proper light. However, their inseparable and pious bond did raise a few eyebrows in and around the university campus. In fact they were erroneously considered a couple. Only the three of them knew the truth.

Reema and Swikriti by now had become frequent weekend visitors. They would spend the day watching films, preparing recipes and sometimes doing their assignments.

Once Hari had been down with malaria and Reema had nursed him endearingly.

Hari and Reema had become so close that the absence of either of them would make the other incomplete. Their care for one another had grown manifold; as if that was the best thing they could do off-late.

Their intense companionship once made Reema vent out, "Why didn't you come earlier in my life?" "Why have we turned out to be so close in no time; and why do we talk so much over the phone?" Hari would be rendered speechless.

*

Once again after a stressful week of university chore, they decided to relax themselves with booze. It had been four months since they last drank together. The arrival of Swikriti's boyfriend set the ideal stage.

It was already nine when they started boozing. They played cards. By now Reema had promoted herself from a mere spectator to one of the good players of *marriage*, thanks to Hari. In no time Swikriti was down and out and Sonam, her boyfriend could not help but take her to sleep. He too had met his quota, it seemed. Reema though had quite a good capacity when it came to booze. Hari was not far behind! There were still two bottles left and they decided they wouldn't sleep without finishing them.

That night, both spoke their hearts out. Yet again Kavita was the topic of discussion. Hari ended up being emotional as he went on sharing the chapters of his once much coveted saga of love and adversity. Reema stared at him with pitiful eyes and embraced him in consolation. A little ease in the emotionally stirring atmosphere urged Reema to open one of the bottles and pour its invigorating content in their respective glasses. By the time they had emptied the bottle, both were leaning against each other for support.

"What should we do with the last one?" Hari asked.

"Finish it," She said conclusively and they both hi-fived.

Reema and Hari now sat in absolute proximity with their backs against the wall, holding hands and talking endlessly. Reema in her dizziness happened to rest her head on his chest. He could feel her breath and she could feel his heartbeat which only got heavier with every passing second. Reema nuzzled him, raised her head and looked at him. Their eyes met and in an impulse their lips met in an inevitable interlock. Reema suddenly pushed him away! He felt awkward and couldn't look at her. In utter guilt he covered his face! Reema got up and left the room. Hari didn't know what to do; he grabbed the bottle and emptied half the content at once. The last gulp nearly made him puke.

Reema returned after a while with a grave look on her face. She must have contemplated long and hard about the unexpected happening. The room was enveloped in an awkward silence.

"Reema," said Hari without looking at her, "I am so sorry. I really didn't intend to do it okay. It just happened."

"It's okay. I understand but let's end this right here; we will not talk about it ever again."

This made him feel a little comfortable. He shared the remaining beer with her in silence. It was soon one in the morning and they decided to sleep. Their eyes met once again and in an impulse they embraced each other and ended up kissing, more passionately this time. He took her in his arms helping her to bed. He slowly laid her down still kissing her deeply and as natural as it seems, his hand caressing her bosom. She held his hand tightly and said, "He loves me a lot, and I love him too. I can't do this to him." She gently slid herself away from him and turned her back towards him. He didn't know what to say so he held her in his embrace from behind. They slept together that night. It was an inexplicable situation that they were in. Swikriti was totally unaware of the turn that had just taken place. Was it right or not? None knew as it was difficult to assess the whirlwind of emotions that had just swept them over.

Humans are the epitome of imperfections, yet
some sins exist which makes us more humane

Chapter XXIV

Stained Joy

A mistake had been committed and now there was no looking back nor could they rectify it. He or rather they slowly and steadily but unknowingly became entangled in a protracted love triangle. Their relationship grew gradually, but now it was a relationship without a name nor future unless they took a drastic step and defied morality.

Meanwhile Hari was selected for a two week workshop on research methodology.

He was to leave for Delhi the following day and they were engrossed in their 'newly usual' messaging affair; the date was 7 May. By now they had started sending love messages and had started wishing each other with goodnight kisses. For few weeks they felt guilty. Both didn't want to eat the forbidden apple, but they just couldn't help it. They even tried to separate ways and every time they tried, they ended up being closer than ever. After numerous attempts, they decided to leave it on time and flow with the flow.

Hari that night in one of his messages wrote, "Hey do you really love me?"

"I luv u..nd dnt think dat I sud be screaming ma heart out."

Hari wrote, "I luv u 2 and m gona miss u.. tak cre."

"Luv u nd will b missin u more.. u to take cre..mmmuuuhhh," She replied.

Another message popped simultaneously, "I think u should sleep now, u hav 2 wake up early tomorw..nd safe journey… enjoy the travel… btw I'll be watchin movie nw…Gud nite luv."

*

He was waiting for the cab to the station the next morning when he thought of making a call to let her know that he was about to leave. But then he remembered that she had slept late. So he typed a few lines and inboxed her. Apart from the information of his departure he had also mentioned that he would not be able to talk freely so if she had anything to say, she should text him. Seven students had been selected from various departments and he was the third to be picked from the Sociology department, after Sambhu and Subho.

It was 8:30 am when he joined the group at the station. The train was running late by three hours. Hari sent Reema a message updating her about the delay. Reema had woken up by then. She replied saying that she was missing him dearly and could not imagine attending classes without him. How she wished that she had also applied for the workshop. Actually Swikriti had backed out and Reema as always had simply followed her friend's footsteps, but this time she regretted profoundly.

Perplexed Reema thought to herself – She had never missed anyone so much before, not even her boyfriend whom she loved immensely. She was unable to understand her own feelings. The only thing she knew was that her life would be miserable without Hari. She couldn't just wait for him to get back. She messaged him stating that she would hug him tight and wouldn't let him go, once he would return.

The train eventually arrived at the platform at twelve. Ironically, the slowest train available had been named 'Neelachal *Express*' – there was nothing 'express' about it! As the train chugged past the platform, Hari messaged her,

"M on my way,"

She replied, "Missing ur warm hug…" He smiled to himself. As the train gathered speed, he immersed himself in incessant texting until the network gave in.

It was at four in the evening that his phone vibrated.

She had written, "Do call me up as soon as u switch on ur cell."

The *Reliance* lady must have been giving her the wrong information. He messaged her back stating that his cell had always been on and that it was because of the network problem. "U tak cre will msg u later.. bye.."

At nine Hari messaged her, "hope u had ur food."

"I had ma food proply..k.. nd dnt keep ur stomach empty..n do try to sleep prply..nd lik I've said, don't want to see u lean n weak when u return.. take cre.. luv u loads."

They reached Delhi after a prolonged journey. The workshop was to be held in Noida but they decided to stay in Delhi overnight. They checked in into a decent hotel and Hari chose to stay alone for obvious reasons. That night he spoke to Reema for a very long time, exchanging sweet nothings. They knew that they were taking a wrong turn which seemed at that moment, the most beautiful turn.

*

They reached Noida the next evening. After the formal registration, they were allotted separate rooms. His classes were to begin the next day. In the morning, he woke up to a message from her.

"Life is too complicated. Don't try to find the answers because when you find the answers, life changes the questions.. strange but true.. good morning.. luv u.."

He brushed his teeth, took a shower and went downstairs to have his breakfast. Subho and Sambhu were waiting for him; they had their breakfast together after which they headed towards Hall - I as they were directed. The whole day they learnt about methodology and its essence in research.

At lunchtime, he checked his cell and read her message, "Want to hug u ya..jus luv the way u make me feel so warm.."

After an attentive week, his patience started to wear off as all he could think of was to be by Reema's side.

Enough was enough! he decided to do the undone – he bunked the classes, hired a rickshaw to the metro station and bought a ticket for Sarojini Nagar.

He messaged her, "hey m in the market… what do u want me to bring for u!"

"Nothing, just come back soon… You know I am missing you so much," Was her demand.

"Ok then I will buy you nothing…"

To which she replied, "Please don't over shop for me."

"Why do you always spoil my Surprises?"

"Because you are so unsurprising… By the way we are planning to have wine, should I have?" She asked.

His laughter in the form of a smiley emoticon that beeped in her cell phone screen was an answer enough. He then contemplated for a while. His trip to Delhi had proved to be a milestone in itself; it had brought them so close that he could hardly imagine. Then he remembered what Swikriti had told him in his first visit to their room. But there was this same girl who was now feeling for a guy so different, in a way so different.

He ended up over shopping for Reema. Then he remembered how Kavita used to end up buying loads for him and would sometimes forget to get anything for herself. Probably she might have had the same feeling as he had at that moment.

By the way she had traversed his mind after a long time. He wondered where she might be and what she might be doing. He wondered whether she remembered him. Deep down in his heart he knew she must have missed him at least sometimes if not always. His thought was disrupted by a message from Reema.

"Just reachd room.. nyway wat u duin?"

He gave the details of his whereabouts and the things he had bought for her. She called him up. He disconnected it and called her back.

"Why did you buy so many things? I had told you not to! Why don't you listen to me?"

He just diverted the talks. After a while he hung up. Then he boarded a metro to Noida and took a vacant seat and resumed his contemplation. Again a message intruded his thoughts,

"Hey! m having 'Dairy Milk Silk', the one u gave me on 14th Feb.. feels so good to have chocolate when feeling hungry.. newy thanx for it.. tak cre..mmuuaahh."

> *Within you I lose myself. Without you I find myself*
> *wanting to become lost again – Unknown*

Chapter XXV

Strepsils

14 February 2009, few weeks after that night when they had slept together, they had decided to spend their day together but they couldn't do it alone as it would confirm the ever-growing suspicion. Hari wanted to make the day special but couldn't think of anything grand. Reema and Swikriti had come to his room. He had bought a Cadbury chocolate and a book. He gave it to Reema when Swikriti had gone to the washroom and had stolen a quick kiss.

It was not a novel or a love story that he gave. It was an Oxford edition on Post Colonialism. What was its essence?? She had to write her assignment on post colonialism and was finding it difficult to procure the right materials.

Swikriti expressed her desire to have pizza. Hari returned to the room half an hour later with a mushroom pizza and a bottle of Coke. Reema chose not to have the Coke owing to her throat-ache. Hari prepared coffee for her. The whole day was spent in rigorous gossiping.

In the evening Swikriti had a dinner date with her boyfriend so Hari and Reema decided to drop her off to the market and then go for some shopping. Her throat ache bothered her all the way. As they got down Hari told the girls that he needed to buy some cigarettes and asked them to wait at the market entrance. He came back with a file of '*Strepsils*', a throat ache remedy lozenges.

The announcement stating the arrival of Noida station made him revert to the present. As he took the rickshaw ride to his lodge, he thought of the 14 February Reema's message to him. He had read it time and again and remembered it by heart, almost.

"Thank u so very much…it's just so thoughtful of u… u realy did understand the need of the hour. But u know what the sweetest thing was?? U buyin me strepsils… felt so much then… u really made me understand that its actually the small things which ultimately means a lot and most importantly thank u for understandin me and my unspoken words. Really fall short to express how glad and fortunate I am 2 hav cum across a beautiful person lik u.. really luv the way you make people feel so warm and special."

A smile flashed on his lips as he remembered it. He had reached his destination.

> *A compliment is something like a kiss*
> *through a veil – Victor Hugo*

Chapter XXVI

The Insignia

The Workshop finally got over. On the last day, they had a valedictory and certificates were awarded. As soon as the day's event was over, he took no time to leave and boarded a metro to New Delhi. The other students who were scheduled to return after three days, planned to go around the capital city as tourists and shoppers.

He had shopped for everyone, for his parents, his near and dear ones, me and most of all, for her. All in all there were ten items exclusively for her and two for Swikriti. There was no way that he could have given those to her in Swikriti's presence. So he thought he would ask her to come to his room.

He went to the travel agency to find the ticket's status but to his dismay his was still in the waiting list. He cancelled his ticket, and got it done from a broker after a hefty payment.

This crazy love! It gets one out of one's senses; out of one's finances. Still the ticket was for the day after. He felt dejected but he had no other option.

He informed her in a despondent mood that he would start the next day to which she replied, "Okay..cheer up ya..things happen for good resons.. luv u dear.."

He slept a sleepless night.

*

Next day at 11:30 am he checked out of the hotel. His bag was heavy but he decided not to hire a coolie. He boarded the train and would reach Kolkata at eleven. There was no way he could meet her and this made him all the more frantic. It was 18 May; Indo-Pak match was on. Despite being a cricket fanatic, he was somehow least bothered about the much TRP raiser as if he knew that it had been fixed.

All his heart and mind was drawn towards that one heart which was helplessly waiting for him.

He reached his room the next day around 10 pm. She would visit him early the next day.

*

A door bell ring at eight in the morning woke him up. He hurriedly went to open the door. There she stood, looking gorgeous in her slinky black attire, a traditional *Kurti* as they say. Things had changed drastically since he had left for Delhi. From just a mere lover his status had been upgraded to something grand; he was now her 'Most Loved Lover'. He had got this insignia during his fourth day of stay in Delhi, he remembered it precisely.

She hugged him instantly and greeted him good morning with a kiss. He withdrew saying that he hadn't brushed as yet but she held on to him and kissed again.

"Just give me a minute okay," He said and went to the bathroom shouting, "And check my bag, the things in the green carry bag belong to you."

He came back drying his hair with a towel only to find the carry bag unopened, untouched. Reema had gone to the kitchen instead, to prepare tea. After a while she came back with two cups of tea along with the snacks she had brought. She opened her backpack and gave him the novel. It was Coelho's 'Brida'.

She was on his lap and tightly embraced in his arms. He could see love in her eyes. She told him about the things she hadn't been able to tell him in detail and he intrigued her with the happenings in Delhi and the markets he had been to where he had witnessed an array of dazzling variety of apparels, and their incredibly low prices. She was thrilled by his narratives. That day they even planned to go to Delhi together some day.

She went after a while as Swikriti wanted her company for that day's visit to the library.

Later that day she messaged:

"M cleanin my closet.. listinin ashes and wine.. missin u.."

Reema would always dedicate some songs and send it to him. The first song she had chosen for him was 'Diamonds and rust' by Joan Beaz, the song Hari would always listen to. The song aptly epitomized the anxiety she felt when Hari would call her up. She once had been very excited to make him hear the song 'Lonely September' and this in fact "explains and encapsulates it all," She had said. "So apt," She would assert; indeed it was. He would feel the same after hearing it. The list went on. He had stacked all the songs given by her in a playlist and would play quite frequently.

Love is when you look into someone's eye and
see everything you need – Unknown

Chapter XXVII

There He Comes

Life just rolled on…amidst love, betrayal and uncertainty.

Four months passed by and it was one of those evenings when Reema sent him an SMS which said, "I don't hav balance, call me up, it's urgent."

He made a call but hung up abruptly and switched off his cell.

Her boyfriend was coming over to see her the next day. He would be reaching by noon. The hotel had already been booked and Reema was to stay with him that night. Hari was feeling uneasy but couldn't stop her from being with him. He knew it was him who had come in between and not Aakash. There was no point in feeling jealous; either he had to end it all and if he chose to continue, he would have had to continue the same way till Reema decided on either of them.

He switched on his cell. There was a flurry of messages first seeking for forgiveness and the latter ones enlightening him about the crude facts,

"You knew everythin rite and I didn't force you to be in the relation we r in. And now u r behaving this way. Ok it was my mistake but m not the only culprit. Just put urself in my shoes and think."

He immediately replied, "I am so sorry for my behavior. Just, wanted to tell you that, I love u a lot. I know u can't evade even if u want to. But I am in no better plane…it really feels miserable. Do go and stay but please don't cross the limits."

She replied, "M sorry, it's just that u become impossible sometimes."

*

Next morning he went to her place. Reema had finished all her errands and was selecting the dress she would wear. Everything she did, especially her last minute preparations fuelled his jealousy all the more.

He asked Reema, "Have you had your breakfast?"

"No," She replied.

"Why not, don't you feel hungry today?" He remarked sarcastically.

"No, not at all," She said to compound to his misery. "Come on Hari, don't behave this way. I believe we had an understanding yesterday."

He didn't know what to say. He just went outside and came with few eggs and a packet of plain bread. He went to the kitchen to prepare the breakfast.

There he was in the kitchen, preparing breakfast for the one he had fallen for. Ironically it was the time when she was going to meet her man. His mind was engrossed in what lay ahead—an eddy of loneliness. Something inside him made him look at the door and there she was smiling at him. That smile was not ordinary, whether it was accompanied by pain or love or may be both he couldn't decipher. He looked at her with an agonizing smile. And she came forward and hugged him. He felt a strange pain within.

After breakfast he wished her *good* day and went back to his room.

That night at about nine she messaged him, "Hey I am wid him bt m misin u so much..tc.."

He wanted to reply but it was too risky he thought and so he refrained from ventilating his tsunami of emotions. That night he missed her; he missed her never ending text messages and their long calls. He would think of what she might be doing. What if she was making love to him; how would he know?

Then he remembered things of his lost love.

Many years back he remembered the night when Kavita had suddenly told him, "Hari I want to confess one thing."

"What?" He had asked.

"I am not a virgin."

He had felt so dejected, but had hugged her tight and had said, "It's ok dear, never mind. I still love you the way I used to. In fact, I have more respect for you now for your honesty."

She had been moved hearing these words but had said, "I have one more thing to tell."

"Now what?" He asked expecting a bigger set back.

"I… I was just testing you, I am still a virgin."

In the next moment he remembered how she had asked him to make love to her to which he had refrained from initially. He also remembered the first time he had made love to her. Ah! That feeling, that pain, how she had closed her eyes and bit her lips. How her finger nails had buried deep into his back. How his body had shivered. Much later she would tell him, "I loved giving myself to you, in fact, I feel privileged and proud."

His thoughts reverted to the present as he thought of Reema. She had revealed to him her prized secret of gifting her chastity to Aakash on his twenty fifth birth day. He also knew that the two would make love whenever they met. So even if they were doing it right now it would just be another time. Then he realized the futility of the last line which he had written in his message the previous day.

In fact, he realized that he had attached undue importance to it; though being able to hold on to people is much more important. Then he thought, he had Kavita's chastity forever just like she had his, but he had lost her now. Next moment he thought what the scenario would have been if Kavita was still with him. Would he have fallen for Reema? And if so what would the situation be? He felt a chill. This thought actually made him understand Reema's predicament in a proper light. He felt at ease now and this particular reflection slowly helped him slip into sleep.

Sometimes all you need is just a right
thought to make things straight

Chapter XXVIII

The Confession

It was June and the results were declared. Swikriti had topped the class; Reema and Hari too had done well. NET exams were round the corner. It was due to be held on the last week of the month. Most importantly her birthday was approaching; the month was thus, bound to be very hectic, an eventful one too.

Hari wanted to celebrate the birthday together, just the two of them; but it was impossible with Swikriti around. It was their last year in Kolkata and presumably his last chance. Something had to be done and done quickly. First they thought of crafting a white lie; informing Swikriti that Aakash had come and Reema would be staying with him. But this was very risky, what if by chance Aakash calls Swikriti? They did have each other's number. After much thought and consideration they finally resolved to speak the truth to Swikriti, rather a part of the truth. Till now they were doing things behind her back. Sometimes things would be very difficult to manage yet doing things secretly bore a peculiar charm. But now the time had come for Swikriti to know the truth, both realized.

*

In one of the evenings Reema held Swikriti's hand and said, "Hey I need to talk to you…I have been hiding something from you."

"What?" Swikriti's eyes tensed up a bit.

With great difficulty Reema finally uttered in one go, "I have fallen for Hari and he loves me too. I know this is wrong but I just couldn't evade what has happened now. How this friendship turned into love, I don't know and I don't know what to do next!"

Swikriti had least expected this. She was always the one who used to defend their relationship and would always reform those who believed them to be a couple.

"Since how long?" She asked.

"About six months."

This literally shocked and stirred her state of mind. Regaining her composure she said, "I was too foolish not to see the obvious. Many told me about you two being in a relationship. Ah! Come on I always took you people to be good friends with the least of botheration to what rumours had been." Saying this Swikriti released her hands and walked outside the room seeking few moments of repose.

Probably it was Reema's deeply imprinted image of a hyper dedicated girl towards her lover that had acted as a veil in front of Swikriti's loyal eyes. Now, she couldn't even suggest her to carry on as she knew Aakash very well and that he really loved her and above all trusted her so much. On the other hand, she couldn't coax her to stop seeing Hari as it was her best friend's choice and she seemed happier and more complete those days. Moreover, it would only make sense if it was just a start; but they had already lived this way for six months now.

At dinner Swikriti at once expressed herself forthrightly, "See, whatever you are doing, it's just not right! But it's your life and you can do whatever you want. And of course, if you are happy, I have nothing to say."

Reema heaved a sigh of relief.

Even I was worried about the turn of events and had once asked Hari, "Are you sure that her feelings towards you will stay that way. I mean from your talk it seems that she really loves you. But my point is, she loved her boyfriend too but she loves you now. Can you be sure that the same story doesn't repeat again? In reply he just downplayed my doubts. Probably he trusted her too much or it may be that he had too much faith in his love; I could only envisage.

They met at will now.

Few days before her birthday, Reema revealed the plan of spending the night with Hari. She also told her that since it was the last year of their togetherness in Kolkata, Hari wanted to do something special and promised that she would not do anything inappropriate.

I'm an idealist. I don't know where I'm going,
but I'm on my way – Carl Sandburg

Chapter XXIX

The Six Strings and the Letter

25 June, 2009, the following day was her birthday and Hari had already laid the blue print. He was supposed to go at six in the evening and pick her up from her room. He didn't go for the classes as he had some preparations to carry out. He woke up at nine and after doing the needful decided to clean his room. He reshuffled everything; from bed to tables to his closet meticulously. It took him almost two hours. He also cleaned the kitchen. Next he swept his house and mopped it. He was tired and it was already twelve. He reposed for half an hour with Reema's new *dedications* on his earphone. He next grabbed his backpack and set out.

He had enumerated the items to be bought for the day in a piece of paper. He first bought a decent quality wine. Then he bought two wine glasses as he didn't want her to have it in their regular mug; he wanted everything perfect on that special day. He bought a casual t-shirt and a miniature Ganesha cult as preliminary gifts. But he had a grander gift in his mind which he would buy at the very last. He also bought a packet of aromatic candles. Reema liked balloons, he bought them too. Then he would buy some spices as he had planned a dish for her. He bought some flowers and a 'Black Forest' cake.

He was sweating in the scorching Kolkata heat but his enthusiasm could not be deterred by it. He was busy and hadn't even replied to her numerous messages. Time was running out for him and he hadn't written the letter. Today he would write her a letter which he thought would spice things up. At last he went to a music store and bought a guitar as the gift of the day. He thought it would be romantic to strum it for her on her special day.

Everything had been perfectly planned to his satisfaction. The first thing he did after coming to the room was to decorate the guitar cover with a bow and hid it behind his closet. He hid the flowers, the candle and the balloons too. It was already five and he had just an hour at his disposal. Initially he wanted to do all the cutting and other culinary preparations before he left but it was not possible. More so he had to write a letter.

He sat down to write but the right words were not just blurting out. It was already six. Finally after wasting a good number of pages he was able to jot down a few lines. But he was not satisfied. Normally he could write volumes but today his pen lacked elegance, maybe out of nervousness, he thought. He folded the letter, covered it with another piece of paper and sealed it.

It was 6:30 pm by the time he reached. Reema had been waiting for him. The three chatted for a while. Swikriti prepared tea for him after which they left.

"Wow! The room looks really clean; it seems someone has taken lots of pain," She said with excitement.

"Even the quilt cover, bed sheets and pillow covers have been changed today itself," He said, in case she would fail to notice.

"So, sweet of you," uttered she with a contended inspection.

It was already 8:30 and he just had a little over three hours to wind up his preparations. Hari said, "Ok dear you take rest now. And yes you are not allowed to come to the kitchen. Just be here okay!"

"But why?" She asked.

"Actually it's a trend we established in Siliguri."

"What trend?"

"We don't let the Birthday ones work on their birthdays."

She was about to protest when he said, "Please dear do as I say." He handed her the much sought DVD, his first surprise though he had forgotten to get the tissue papers.

The latest Korean Movie collection brought her so much joy as if she had got a bottle of beer on a dry day.

He had planned to prepare various recipes and a special dish which he had created for her, the *Recapchee*; this was supposed to be the biggest surprise. He started his preparations. In between he would go and sit near her and would steal a quick kiss from her salty cheeks, thanks to Korea. By 11:20 he was done with his cooking and was all set to manage the surprise.

"Okay now you have to go to the other room and let me arrange a few things; take the laptop with you and please don't argue, we don't have time." She gave him a tearfully impatient smile as she adhered to his directions. Thanks to Korea again.

He locked the door from outside and cleaned the room once again. He spread a profile on the floor, placed a mattress on top of it and covered it with a bed sheet. He then inflated all the balloons with utmost circumspection. The neat room was filled with balloons of different colors. Next he placed the cake on the table. He then brought the gifts, the wine and the other things.

"How long will it take?" enquired the anxious voice from the other room.

"I'm just there sweetheart," He answered and hurried things up.

It was all done, the wine glasses had been equally filled; the lights had been switched off and the candles were illuminating the room thereby making the temperature to shoot up all the more. The plates were decorated with a variety of delicacies. He scanned carefully if he had missed out on anything. He purposely kept the guitar concealed and this would be the last surprise. Still fifteen minutes were left of the tedious though exciting 25 July.

"Now stop crying, it's almost twelve and I don't want you to cry this time… the way you have been," Said Hari sliding down the laptop screen.

"Ok," She said with a forlorn smile.

"Promise?"

"Promise!"

10…9…8…7…6 and 5. She was now twenty-two years, three hundred sixty four days, twenty three hours and fifty five minutes old.

He brought her to the room with his hands covering her eyes.

As he uncovered her eyes she exclaimed in delight, "Wow!" She hugged him and planted a kiss on his forehead standing on her toes. He led her to the cake which read '*To my beloved, happy b'day*'. At the stroke of twelve she cut the cake and he hummed the happy birthday tune. She cut a piece and fed him first, he fed her the other half.

Meanwhile her boyfriend called her up and she signaled with a finger on her lips to remain quiet. Hari felt miserable first for himself and bit later for the guy. She chatted for just a while and hung up the phone. She would pick no other calls that night. Now he gave her the gift which when opened brought her to elation. She instantly went to the other room to try the t-shirt; it was a perfect fit. He felt relieved and happy. He then handed her a red rose, the letter and the other flowers.

"This is the best birthday ever," She cried out jubilantly.

Very anxiously, she opened the envelope and read the letter:

"Dear Reema,

Meeting you has been one of the momentous happening of my life. You just don't know how happy and glad I am to have met you. It's amazing that within such a short span of time you have captured both my heart and soul. Thank you so much for coming into my life and also for bestowing me with such precious moments.

Also I would like to take the opportunity to say sorry for the times I have hurt you for not understanding your sacrifices and your predicaments. But the greatest truth is that I love you. You have given me new wings to fly high in love and I am really thankful to the almighty for sending you for me. On this special moment, let me wish you a very happy birthday. May all your wishes come true, may you remain happy forever and may we be together always."

She didn't speak; she carefully dropped the letter on the decorated table as they hugged each other long and tight; they stood in silence.

"Our drink is getting cold," He said trying to be humorous. She smiled and they sipped their wine. He had already created a playlist which he played from his phone. They chatted for a while munching the snacks that he had prepared.

"And this I invented especially for you and I have named it *Recapchee*," He said forwarding a plate of his indigenous recipe. To Reema's query he explained – 'Re' symbolized her name initials; 'cap' stood for capsicum, one of the chief ingredients of the dish and 'chee' meant cheese another ingredient. At last he de-camouflaged the prized gift and handed it to her.

She said in an exhilarated tone, "Awww! Thank you so much. O! O! It's wonderful."

The candles and the switched off fan turned the room unbearably hot. The ambience would have been perfect for cold places, but the searing conditions of Kolkata would not let his romantic endeavor last long. They decided to switch on the light and the fan keeping the candles at bay. The humidity made them sweat profusely and they decided to take shower. Hari went in first and came back quickly. Reema asked Hari to give her some clothes to change. He gave her a green t-shirt and a white pair of cotton trousers. She came back at once.

Hari asked, "Hey what happened? You don't want to take a shower?"

"The bathroom walls are so dirty; I can't keep the clothes hanging there."

"*Chhya*! How could I forget to clean that? I wanted everything perfect but…. I am sorry."

"No it's ok; I will change in the room itself," Said she and left for the bathroom taking only the towel with her. Hari cleaned up the room and disposed the garbage. After a while she came to the room with just the towel draped around her body, her shoulders and her lovely thighs well exposed. The water dripping from her hair left tiny little beads on the shoulders making her appear really attractive, in fact nubile. He could not take his eyes of her. The sight ignited Hari's wild guise. He could not control his desire, so he swept her in his arms and started kissing her. The fragrance of the shampoo was the aphrodisiac for him and he pulled her even closer; close enough for her to feel his throb.

He gently kissed the nape of her neck thereby sucking up the water that was hindering its touch with the skin. The disrobed towel lay discarded on the floor, exposing her curvaceous body. They could feel each other's warmth clenched in one body. The eternal love which they now felt for each other blossomed. Now there was no guilt. No remorse. All there was, was a deep animal hunger to ravish each other. She lay down and he was above her. His strokes were gentle at first and then it started rocking speedily. Both were breathing heavily and sweating when they reached their orgasm.

Later they slept in each other's arms cuddled up together under one blanket.

His letter, now her letter still lay fluttering on the table probably smiling back at Hari.

Nothing is worth more than this day –
Johann Wolfgang von Goethe

Chapter XXX

A Walk in the Rain

Next evening, Reema took Hari and her friends to a restaurant for her birthday treat. They ordered for starters and drinks and Hari opted for whiskey. They were having a good time when Reema received a call from Aakash. She excused herself and went aside to speak to him. Long anxious moments passed by but Reema didn't return. He gulped down his fifth peg and went looking for her. He found Reema facing the wall, engrossed in the conversation. Hari stood un-noticed.

As she hung up she whispered, "I love you like no one else my baby, can't wait to see you." She turned around just to find herself in a face off. She understood that Hari had overheard their conversation which left her petrified. Nervousness was writ all over her wintry face. Hari was blazing within, still trying to understand her but he couldn't harmonize. He went near and hissed into her ears, "I am going…going away from your life," and he left the restaurant.

It was drizzling when he got out. He thought of hiring a taxi but chose to walk instead. He felt drops of rain penetrating gradually from his hair to his face to his body. The drizzle suddenly turned into a downpour. He felt relieved as the rain got harder and hit his head with magnitude. He got thoroughly drenched but that mattered least at the moment. The stinging pain that arose made his heart heavy and he found it difficult to breathe. He then felt warm tears trickle down his cheeks and momentarily became conscious of his surroundings. But then again, he did not care; he started crying in the rain. He thought of his uncertain future with Reema and felt hopeless. He thought he would never come back to her but his heart shuddered from the idea of living a lonely life once again.

With such conflicting thoughts he entered his room drenched to the skin. He pulled out his cell phone from the pocket; thank god the waterproof cover had prevented the damage. There were thirty nine missed calls, twenty five from Reema and rest from others. He knew he had spoiled her birthday. It was only yesterday that he had given her the moment of a lifetime and today he had ruined it all. She would cry today also, he thought. How he wished he hadn't got that drunk and behaved the way he did. He wanted to respond to her calls but decided not to; he was heartbroken too. He wiped his phone and removed the moist; kept his phone in the silent mode; dried himself up and went off to sleep. The alcohol acted as a tranquilizer and he slept sound.

*

He woke up early in the morning. He was feeling thirsty and his head was aching a bit. He took few gulps of water, felt a little better and sat on the chair. The events of yesterday flashed back in his memory. He realized he really needed a break; he decided to go back home in the evening itself. His hands reached out for his phone. There were another ten missed calls from her and a message. She had written,

"M so sorry I cudn't keep the promise of not cryin…like I said I do every time on my b'day.. m missin u so so much.. so much.. the time spent wid u certainly was the best time I had in 23 years of my life and it certainly will remain cherished forever.. will miss those moments forever. Thanx for coming to my life and making me feel like the most special one in the whole wide world..and loving me like no one before.. u as a person will forever be loved, missed and respected.. m sorry for all the trouble and the pain and making your life so difficult.. lastly I'll always be loving you forever and always.. tak cre and hav ur food well.."

He chose not to reply though he wanted to. He was lost in contemplation when he heard a soft knock at his door. Who could it be so early in the morning? He thought. He went to open the door and to his guess it was her. Later Swikriti would reveal how she had cried all night thinking that he had gone away from her life and how she would miss him, his love and his cares.

She at once said, "Please don't leave me."

He, after a moment of silence said, "I love you a lot but I don't think I will be able to continue this way. Yesterday I heard your talks with him, then I realized how much you love him and I am the one in between. Things have happened between us that cannot be undone but I guess we can live with that. I know you love him and you love me too but you'll have to make a choice one day and deep down inside I feel I should be the one to help us out of this impasse."

But she would say, "It just blurted out, I really didn't mean it," and further asserted, "I can imagine my life without him, but I can't imagine my life without you; please don't leave me." She hugged him and everything was back to the fairy tale again. The pain he was feeling seemed to have diluted with that embrace of hers.

A hug overcomes all boundaries. It speaks words
within the mind that cannot be spoken —Unknown

Chapter XXXI

The Option that Mattered

They became closer than ever especially after that momentous night that they had spent together.

Their talks and their stays increased. Now even Aakash found her phone engaged most of the times and had started complaining. He presumed that there was something between Hari and Reema. This he had imbibed as she would sometimes subconsciously designate Aakash as Hari during conversations. This in fact became the bone of contention between the two which transcended into their regular mix ups and fights.

To multipart Reema's misery further, Hari had been insisting her to make a choice between him and Aakash. Poor Reema was torn in between; she didn't know what to do and what not to. She couldn't leave Aakash for Hari as she knew he would be devastated but couldn't help herself not falling for Hari more and more. She at that point of time couldn't imagine her life without Hari.

In fact, she had been realizing for quite some time that her feelings towards Aakash had diminished largely and she was hardly excited in seeing him anymore. Earlier she would make all the efforts to end their fights with her 'first moves' but now she hardly bothered. Aakash was habituated to her first moves and was complacent as always. Little did he know that he no longer thrived in her heart as he used to; most of it had been occupied by Hari.

When she couldn't figure out what to do, she talked about the matter to Swikriti, who would only profess that there was no way rectifying things now as a lot had been shown and done.

Two options lay before her. She could either go back to Aakash or choose Hari. What was being done to Aakash was not fair. Reema had cheated the one who trusted her with all his heart. It was just not right to let him be a mere spectator of his own doom. She had already committed a *crime* but the only practical and viable *verdict* left for her would be to choose Hari. Either ways she would be feeling guilty, no doubt, but at least Hari knew the truth and had already accepted her. But Aakash was blind to the things happening behind his back. The day he would find out, God knows what would happen.

After much contemplation Reema finally decided to end her relation with Aakash. After all, for how long can one decide to stand on two boats at the same time?

On the other side little did Aakash know that the doubt he had harboured would culminate in their breaking apart.

He however, couldn't imagine his life without Reema and wanted her back no matter what. He felt that their breakup was the consequence of his inability to give her much time. Still he hoped against hope that he was not given up for another guy. He resolved to take all necessary steps to get her back. He then initiated his mending pursuits. He regularly called Reema seeking for forgiveness. He promised to give her enough time henceforth. At first Reema avoided, but his regular calls made her susceptible at times.

When Aakash understood that the matter was not progressing enough, he approached Swikriti for help. Swikriti on the other hand only remained a helpless observer of the entire situation. Reema at times felt guilty that she left Aakash for no fault of his. She felt all the more penitent when he regularly asked for forgiveness. Moreover, Swikriti's constant spur was igniting to Reema's indecisiveness.

*

It was amidst such emotional turmoil that one evening Reema informed Hari that she was wanted home urgently. Hari offered to accompany her but she declined. Instead she asked him to get the ticket confirmed the next day. Luckily he succeeded in securing a three tier A/C ticket for her. They once again stayed together that night. She expressed her desire to booze. They drank more than usual. That night Hari had felt really strange. He was feeling a void even with her around.

Hari had then questioned Reema

"What if we can't make it all the way?"

She had said, "If I can't marry you, I would miss your absence madly and I would always be jealous of your wife." She had abruptly added, "Please take care always." She had cried hugging him tight. Hari felt, it was her excess intake that had made her emotional.

They became one—one soul.

> *Why can't choices be as simple as tea*
> *or coffee... whiskey or beer*

Chapter XXXII

Shadows and Reflections

The knot when tied more than once gets so tight that it becomes difficult to loosen.

The next day he went to drop her to the station and stayed with her till the train left the platform. She reached Siliguri after a ten hour journey and informed that she would be heading home straight. She messaged twice in between informing about her inability to message him regularly. Her relatives were home and more importantly she would be sleeping with her mom.

Hari was still hopeful of that 'one call' till ten. He couldn't sleep as it was 'their' hour. But today there would be no good night kisses, no lovely words and no Reema. He was on his bed trying to curtail his anxiety and he remembered their trip to Delhi together. This time it was for a two day seminar on environment. Though they had little interest on the topic, they had applied just to fulfill their dream which they had seen in Hari's room.

They had a great time there; had shopped a lot. Reema had bought him a horoscope book and a black shirt.

He remembered how she had fallen ill during their return and how he had cared for her. The co-passengers from Bihar had remarked, "*Bahut pyar hey in dono mein*" meaning, "they have much love between them." Hari had kept her in his arms all the time and he cuddled her like a child. Reema had preserved a hundred rupee note given by Hari as a souvenir. It brought a smile to his face much later when she had shown him calling it the 'Train Note'.

He unlocked his cell and clicked the message icon. There were 2863 messages in the folder 'Diamonds and rust'. He browsed through few of her messages and their pictorial memories of their stay in Delhi. Gradually he fell asleep in the endeavor of his contemplation.

*

He woke up in the morning. He at once checked his phone for her message. He did find one. It was not Reema, but the network provider informing him of the best tariffs.

This was something which had never happened. He was startled but later began to worry. Random, pessimistic thoughts occupied his mind making him restless.

He called her up but she didn't receive. After five attempts he finally gave up. He tried after ten minutes; still she didn't take up his call. After fifteen minutes he tried again but in vain. He was enraged by her lack of response. He switched off his cell but quickly switched it on. Still no messages were to be found. At last her message popped at about eleven. "Sorry was busy. Good morning, take cre and hav a wonderful day," that was it. It had been hours since he hadn't heard her voice and holy God! He desperately wanted to. This was really strange. He thought he would go to Swikriti and find out whatever he could. He knew he would get something or the other.

The next day before going for classes, he went to Swikriti's room. He asked whether she had been able to talk to her; to which she said 'No'. He told her how she had not called him for a day now.

"What's the matter," He asked.

"I don't know… she must be busy I guess," She said casually.

"Swikriti, I know you are hiding something from me. Please I deserve to know and I have the right too," He said in a prerogative tone.

"Hari, I told her to let you know but she doesn't want to tell you what can I possibly do?"

"Don't beat around the bush, just tell me the truth."

"She has gone to her boyfriend."

He felt numb as he heard the news. He felt as if the ground beneath him had just slipped away.

"Thanks" he said and left.

He couldn't understand why she had to lie; and if she wanted to go back to Aakash why was she behaving the way she was with him. He then remembered her words, "I can imagine my life without him but I can't imagine my life without you." He just couldn't understand her stance. He needed answers to his queries and he needed it there, at that very moment.

He called her numerous times but she did not attend to his call. A sudden thought made him browse the contact list and dialed Aakash's number. He was saved no more as 'Reema's sky' but just Aakash. He would talk to her today no matter what, he thought. He just wanted to ask Reema whether she wanted to be with him or her boyfriend. The answer was obvious but still he wanted to hear it in the face. Actually it was her lie that was hurting him more than anything else. Aakash's cell was switched off. He kept trying and trying and finally got the call through.

"Hello?" the husky voice on the other side said.

"Hello!" Hari replied. "Can I talk to Reema? It's somewhat urgent… regarding her studies," He said trying to sound normal.

"Who are you?" He asked assertively.

"It's Hari."

"Oh! So it's you…Actually I wanted to talk to you for long but Reema doesn't let me talk to you. I think there's something between Reema and you, what is it? I can sense it as it is after your arrival in her life that our relationship has strained."

Hari said, "There's nothing as you think, now can I please speak to her?"

"It can't be. Come on tell me the truth," Hari kept mum.

Aakash further asked, "Since how long?"

The question came rather out of the blue to Hari.

Hari still wanted to keep mum but words just blurted out, "About a year!" All had been said and done; those three words from Hari had changed three lives in a moment.

In a way this was inevitable; it would come about one day or the other. The only difference was that it had come about at such a moment when no one, not even Hari had expected.

Aakash felt a storm. He stood motionless. A sudden rush of blood raced towards his head. He turned the room helter-skelter as he threw things around in his rage. He knew how much she loved him but couldn't understand why she had to do it. He had done no wrong and had not cheated upon her.

Later that evening Reema called Hari.

As soon as he picked up the phone she said, "I hate you; you hear I hate you so much and I regret for all I did. It was only yesterday that he had proposed me for marriage. You have destroyed my life," She emphasized.

He had never expected to hear those words from Reema. With these words from her a chasm had been created in his heart, a chasm difficult to fill up.

"Why did you lie to me and why didn't you pick up my calls. If only you had told me the truth and had picked up at least once..." He sighed.

"Why did you call him up?" She counter questioned. Suddenly all the respect and love with which she always talked to him had vanished; she was becoming assertive.

"You left me with no choice. Just call someone as many times as I did! And when you don't get a response, then you will understand how I felt!" But she was in no mood to understand and they hung up the phone.

All he knew was that the things would not be the same again.

*

A week passed by after this incident. Hari was in his room waiting for Subho who would come to take few readings from him. The bell rang and he went to open the door for him. But little did he know that it would be the *hardest* door opening. There stood Reema, pale and drawn; her face dripping with sweat. The charm and the glow which her beautiful face had always inherited had suddenly been ransacked. She came close to him and unexpectedly embraced him; he didn't know how to react. He maintained a façade of indifference. He wanted to tell her how penitent he felt but again had a few queries to which he needed explanations; he just kept mum. But he was surprised as to why she had come to the one who had destroyed her life. It was she who broke the jinx.

"He was ill and pleaded me to come." It didn't matter to him whether it was a true or not; he wouldn't be able to trust her the way he blindly did.

Trust is very precious and it's like a glass, once you break it you can never regain it no matter how hard you try; the *scar* still remains.

Reema cried and hugged him again. A door bell made her withdraw and this time it was Subho. She bid him goodbye and went out of the room.

Later that evening he took out his diary and wrote.

"The void inside seems too large, can't figure out what stuff it's made of. Is it the outcome of my loss or is it that I am feeling too large for somebody else. But deep down inside, the loss still rankles. I am very well aware of it, still, even now when I realize it; it pinches me an extra bit. Again I come to my old paralyzed state, the most apt place it seems for me; probably to the world which I belong. But yes that doesn't sum up. Really it's so hard to see tears in those eyes which are too precious. How I wish those were mine; how I wish I could do the honour. Then I couldn't but I am doing it now, as I write these lines. You feel the tears rolling down those eyes but really can't find the right words to console. In the process you lose an opportunity to tell how equally bad you feel and most importantly "please don't cry, I can't afford to see the tears in your eyes; I surely will be there in your dark hours." But you fear to utter those lines because you know you aren't special anymore and even if uttered, they will sound no more than a mere line. She needed, I felt a better company, the one she really loved; who'd console her much and bring those smiles right back to her face and in her life and in no time. How happy she would have been to know that the person who means the most is very well beside you. Alas! Couldn't even give it to her knowing very well what she wanted. It's ironic that the person whom you love can only be happy with your tears. Now is there a difference between tears and happiness? And you have no option but to let go and to cry and cry after that, so that the others stay happy forever. Now you begin to ask yourself can you live it that way. The heart replies yes for sure, anything for you dear; I really love to see you happy."

With his heart penned down, he felt a little at ease. Next he decided that he would never look back again. He didn't call her after that. He now wanted to believe that whatever she was feeling for him was not love… at least. He realized that their relationship had already died its death.

Love is the most used at the same time misused word in any language. Some feelings remain which are lesser than love and higher than friendship, and we suffer to express it because we lack that proper word. And many times young hearts are caught up in such a net where they can get in without learning to get out of it. And when one comes out, after the destruction of one's world, one cannot firmly stand. They stagger for a long time, fearing their own shadows, their own reflections.

I believe that everything happens for a reason. People change so that you can learn to let go, things go wrong so that you can appreciate them when they are right…and sometimes good things fall apart so better things can fall together – Marilyn Monroe

Part III

Chapter XXXIII

A Month in Sikkim

The year was 2010. Hari completed his M.Phil and returned home. He was determined to work and immediately started hunting for jobs. His uncle in U.S. had been urging Hari to join him and try his luck abroad. But he was someone who didn't like going out of his country, rather his hometown. After a month's hunt he got placed in one of the leading NGOs in Darjeeling which addressed issues related to human trafficking.

It was also the time when Darjeeling was boiling in turmoil and was grappled with *bandhs* and strikes as the Gorkhaland movement had just been revived in the hills yet again.

The movement was considerably gaining momentum since its inception in 2007 by a newly formed party. Initially, a temporary settlement had been reached between the state authorities and the party in the form of a much promising agreement. 'Darjeeling hills' was to be developed and in fact to be made the Switzerland of India. Ironically, the Switzerland promise brought only the snow and with it, *snow fights*. The development agreement was unable to satisfy the long and pending demand of the Gorkhas and hence the statehood demand had gathered its pace hitherto unheard of.

As such everything was affected; from education to economics and tourism to trade, even the National Highway 31 monkeys. The hardest hit industry was tourism upon which a lot of common people depend their livelihood on.

It was 9 July when serious fall-out took place between the state government and the hill party whereby the latter summoned a total *bandh* from the 11th. Pandemonium broke out as the news of indefinite strike dispersed through the town. Everyone was in a hurry to get back to their homes. The tourists who had come to enjoy the serene beauty of the Darjeeling hills were immediately asked to leave forcing them to cut short their vacation. Hari straight away packed his belongings and booked his ticket home.

Hari knew I was in Kalimpong so he came straight to my house unannounced. We were meeting after a long time and it was customary to chat about many things and of course his love life. He told me about Reema and their subsequent happenings in detail. I learnt that Reema would sometimes give him a call but he never called her. I couldn't discern whether he still loved her or not, but I felt he still had a soft corner for her. But he was reticent about it. Perhaps he just didn't want to hear "you have destroyed my life," yet again. He told me that he had felt really bad hearing those words from her.

I was going to Sikkim, a northeastern Indian state, the next day as my classes were on. I asked Hari to accompany me. He thought it was a good idea but had to seek his parents' permission. He went home after dinner. He called me up in the morning to confirm that he was accompanying me.

Next day he came to my house at about nine. I had been waiting for him to have breakfast together. Like all other moms my mom was worried about me leaving again and the thing that worried her the most was about me not having proper food. Her cooking is always delicious (still not quite like my grandma's) and she had taught me a few of her specialities but I, being a lazy bum, mostly relied on junk foods. Today she had dearly cooked my favourites, rice, *Kalo daal*, cauliflower curry and *Churpi ko achar* which we had with dollops of pure ghee of course.

As I wound up my last minute preparation, we took a local taxi and headed towards the motor stand. We bought tickets at a higher rate, a common trend in the hills when the strikes are declared or called off. As expected there was a dramatic increase in the normal activity. The spectacle so created becomes interesting to observe. People gathered in the motor stand, all in a hurry to get vehicles, some with heavy luggage and some with children around. Everyone had their own reasons to travel that very day and struggled to get the tickets. What a sight, it is! Political parties call strikes within short notice without caring for the reaction of the common people and yet they promise of better things and better situations. Utopia becomes the order of imagination.

During our stay at Gangtok the entire period passed as I kept listening about Hari's past. At times Reema would give him calls which he *un-heartily* ignored. I assumed he was fighting to keep her away from his mind.

On the 15 August the strikes were withdrawn for merely three days. We still went to Kalimpong to witness the traditionally grand Independence Day celebration, but this time, it was not at all close to what it used to be. We returned to Gangtok the very next day.

During our stay together in Sikkim, I remember having a very memorable conversation with Hari when we were drunk. Our talks reverted from Reema and Kavita to our days in Siliguri.

"Hey how are our guys?" Hari had curiously enquired.

"Yeh, they are all doing well, everyone is now employed, I am the lone exception," I said with a smile.

"Aren't you in touch with them?" I asked

"No it's been a long time," Hari contemplated taking a vodka sip.

"And have you all sorted out your differences?" He asked.

"Yah, perhaps everyone realized its futility and guess maturity has played its part," I admitted.

"But you know Hari I have to tell you one thing which I wanted to, I mean that night after the *Court More* incident."

"What?"

"It really hurt me when you refused to take my side."

"I know but I had a reason," He went on.

"You are the first one whom I came to know. In fact, it was because of you I got to stay there and came across the others and that act of mine seemed ungrateful, I know. But you see I can't be ungrateful to Millen and Bristrit, they have done so many good things to me. I remember Bristrit was once suffering from fever yet he accompanied me to the railway station to receive my dad. This is just an example I am giving. And Millen, he was, if you remember, my 'water duty' partner. You know he always carried the heavier jar and left the lighter ones for me. All through my stay there, they have always been there for me. I just didn't want to be ungrateful to them so I chose not to take sides. Now you tell me if I am wrong?"

I stayed mum in retrospection

"Man, always remember, it is these small things which we should always pay heed to. If you have the habit of seeing the small things, you won't miss the bigger ones. I know my philosophies have always bored you…" He smirked.

With another glass of alcohol he was unstoppable,

"To be honest, life will acquaint you with a lot of bad ones too, but if you remember just the bad things they inflicted, then you are for sure, nurturing negative vibes. It will only hamper you in the long run. You know I have had to face a lot of adversities, especially in love. But I never have thought ill about the people who put me into such situations. And it is this very *mantra* that has kept me going."

Once again I even in that drunken state felt like tucking him and his philosophy into a polythene and garbage it into a dustbin.

I said I was done with both the drink and his philosophies and went off to sleep.

Finally the announcements were made that the strikes would be lifted as tripartite talks had been scheduled to assess the demand. Hari decided to go to Darjeeling the very next day.

> *Trying to forget someone you love is like trying to remember someone you never met – unknown*

Chapter XXXIV

Unexpected Turn

Hari went to the ticket counter and to his surprise he knew the ticket counter guy. His association with him had been from the days he stayed in Siliguri.

There in the counter he was waiting for the cab to meet its quota. It was then that a man in his mid fifties approached him. He had flecks of grey hair. He wore a grey-framed bifocal spectacle which matched his expensive grey suit.

"It's taking more than usual right? Are you going to Darjeeling too?" The man asked.

"Yes uncle," He replied.

"What do you do?"

"I work in an NGO," He said and added with a brief pause, "It addresses human trafficking issues."

"Oh good!" The man exclaimed.

The conversation lasted until they were directed towards the cab's parking point. Since Hari had known the ticket counter guy he was allotted the best seat. This was distinctive of him. He always seemed to have good contacts. But all his contacts were not with people from the upper strata but largely with the ordinary ones; he really gelled well with such people. I know he had many Bengali friends in Siliguri; one was a tea maker; other worked at a road side hotel; one worked in his uncle's shop; one was a shoe maker and the other owned a vegetable stall in the heart of Siliguri town. Apart from them he had many friends from college whom he was really close with and I presume he was close to all. He was the one whom anybody could trust and I bet he knew everyone's secret.

Hari was sitting on his window seat at the front. The co-passengers were basically the women folk. One of the ladies at the back was constantly grumbling about her uncomfortable seat. He immediately offered his seat to her which she happily accepted. But later he realized that he had placed himself in the middle of women which made him a little uncomfortable. As he turned around he saw a young girl sitting awkwardly at the last seat. He had not noticed her earlier. She was the daughter of the man he had spoken to a while ago.

He asked her, "Would you like to take my seat? I guess you are feeling uncomfortable."

"No thank you, I am fine," She replied.

Her father suggested her to go but she declined again.

"You don't have to feel awkward, come take my seat," Hari insisted.

"Thank you but I am fine out here," She affirmed.

Yet again he turned towards her to see if she had changed her mind but he couldn't read her face. He presumed that she would regret the lost opportunity later on. Soon the luggage was properly packed at the cab's roof rack and the vehicle started to wheel on. Hari after sometime for an unknown reason happened to look back again only to catch a glimpse of her. She was engrossed in a Sidney Sheldon novel, the title of which he said he couldn't remember.

In a few hours of travel they reached a popular Y-junction, *Teesta* well known for its *Teesta Bridge.* A lady next to Hari directed the driver to stop the cab, her destination had arrived. Hari immediately asked the young lady to come to the vacated seat. This time the girl didn't hesitate. To this Hari thought of abdicating his seat for her father but for some reasons he did not. She was now sitting close to him. The cab started to wheel again. She had stopped reading her novel and was now fiddling with her *Blackberry* phone. From the corner of his eyes he could see that she was using *Whatsapp* and must have been messaging her boyfriend, he thought. This he assumed because once he happened to glance at her phone and she had hurriedly clicked the screen-lock button as if she was hiding some classified information. She was constantly messaging and it was making Hari jealous, for the reasons still unknown.

Hari's phone rang and the sobbing voice on the other side unfolded the catastrophe that had befallen her. Suddenly the composure he had kept all these times began to crumble; it was Reema. He felt bad that her granny had passed away but could do nothing except console her. Moreover, he wasn't finding the right words. How he wished he could do something or say magical lines which would bring those precious smiles right back to her face. He then realized how he still had soft corners for her though it was all over between them.

He did feel strange how she still remembered him during her unfortunate hour. He thought she felt more at ease and more complete with him. This thought made him glad but he also knew that uncertainty would loom over their relationship again, so he dealt with her a little stoically.

Soon her balance got over and the phone got disconnected. Immediately he called her back but this time the network disallowed; he felt frantic and melancholic at once. He kept gazing at his cell and when the network indicator gradually escalated, in an impulse he dialed her number. The voice on the other side was snobbish and cranky, the phone got disconnected again. He redialed it only to discern that he had exhausted his talk time balance. He became impatient and cursed himself for not re-charging the phone. But it was not his fault. Off late he hardly made any regular calls. He just hoped that the cab would halt soon so that he could recharge his account. He knew that the conventional stoppage *Lopchu* was not very far, but it was just not approaching for him today.

The driver raced the engine before it stopped. In *Lopchu* usually the cabs halt for a while; for snacks, lunch or breakfast. More importantly if it's the last trip to Darjeeling, they seize the opportunity to wash their vehicles. As soon as a vehicle approaches, there will be one or the other washer boy ready to do the job. It isn't that laborious, but they must be earning handsomely given the enthusiasm they exhibit in their cleaning. In *Lopchu* finding water is like finding oil in the Gulfs, unlike in Darjeeling, now an hour away, where it's like finding brooks in the deserts.

He got down and before he ordered for tea and snack, went searching for a *Reliance* voucher. He explored the whole lane of shops lined on either side of the road but to his dismay he could find none. He then thought for a while and decided that he would ask somebody close to recharge his account. But for that he needed somebody else's cell phone to enable him a call. Hari felt extremely awkward initiating talks with the strangers hence the only option was the man in the mid fifties who had conversed with him at the ticket counter. Hari approached him and in a hesitant manner asked,

"Excuse me uncle can I use your phone for a call? It's urgent and I could not find *Reliance* voucher out here."

To this the man said, "I am sorry, I forgot to bring my cell phone today."

"But wait," He said and called his daughter and continued, "Lend your cell phone to him; he has an urgent call to make."

He felt awkward and wanted to decline the offer but he had no other choice.

She asked Hari, "Give me your number, I will transfer you the amount... but... is yours *Vodafone*?"

"Nope it's *Reliance*."

"Oh! then take it," She said handing him the phone.

He called me up and asked me the much needed favour. He disconnected the phone and thanked the girl. He was feeling awkward taking help from 'quite a stranger'. He then bought a fag for himself and Rs. 20 *Vodafone* voucher for her to express his gratitude, which he would forget to give it later. As he was smoking the girl came and stood near him. This was the first time he observed her. She had fair skin, was a bit taller than him and was healthily built, yet she wasn't fat or even close to that. She had big dreamy eyes. Her hair was carelessly tied or maybe it was because of her sleep in the cab, he thought. She was pretty and her lips were pink and beautiful. She had a ruddy complexion, so idiosyncratic to the girls of Darjeeling.

He asked, "Are you in college?"

"Everyone asks whether I study in college but I am a student of Loreto Convent School and I am in the 12th standard. I think it is because of my built that people have such opinion about me." She said in one go wearing a serene smile.

At that very moment his cell phone beeped a message tone and he knew exactly what. He asked her to excuse him and made a call to Reema. Soon everyone had finished with food and other needs. The car too was done with its wash.

One thing I have realized is that when you travel in a shared vehicle and stop for a while and get down; when you take your seats again you seem fatter and it becomes congested for a while and it takes some time for things to settle down. They all had become fatter and found themselves very close to each other especially Hari and the Loreto girl. Hari realized that he was sitting very close to the girl and could feel her body against his. He became conscious but he did not want to shift an inch apart.

As they went further the two found themselves all the more close to each other. That day the roads were congested owing to the *meeting* called by the ruling party. The cab was moving at a turtle's pace. Everyone was grumbling except for the two. They were enjoying the closeness that they were experiencing. At times he felt her hand against his but instead of withdrawing he wanted to hold it. He nearly did but checked himself thinking what her reaction would be and it was moreover a very indecent gesture. Neither of them uttered a word; they didn't need to even. The girl checked her phone again and it made him all the more restless; bit jealous and bit hurt; strange but true.

At about eight they reached Darjeeling. He wanted to bid her bye but on what ground he would say; he hadn't uttered a word in the cab. While he got down she was looking at him. She was feeling a strange pain within and this was the first time it was happening with her. She had felt so at ease with him around; she felt an uncanny void as he left. And he stood there for a while trying to understand the situation, he was unable to comprehend himself.

That night his mind was split into two. His mind and heart oscillated between Reema and the girl whom he had just met. He was for some time thinking about how Reema would be feeling. He thought of calling her up but then he remembered the *crushing* line, "You want to destroy my life."

But in another moment he was thinking of the Loreto girl. She was just a few hours old in his memory but certainly the strongest urge at that moment. He couldn't remember her face but he remembered her closeness and her touch. He could feel her head on his shoulders. He felt a sudden urge to talk to her. But how was he supposed to find her, he knew nothing of her except that she was a student at Loreto; an *LC-ite*.

On the other side in one of the corners in Darjeeling the girl was having strange feelings that night. She was thinking of the stranger who had sat next to her close, very close to her. Had she left her heart in that cab? She was thinking.

Hari was desperately trying to remember her face while covering his own. Suddenly he removed his hands and smiled in contentment.

"Man can you pass me the number?" He called me in excitement.

"What number are you talking about?"

"Mmmm....the one I had called you from, today evening."

"Ok! Let me see if I have retained it."

I could sense his gasp as he said "ok!"

Now that he had the number, he thought why was he doing this!! He never had had the urge to ask for the number of any of his female co-passengers though he had found some to be beautiful and attractive. But this girl, he didn't even remember her face. Moreover, what would he say after he called her; what reasons would he give; and what would she think of him. Against all odds he finally decided to call her up but it was already ten and he thought that the timing was inappropriate. The next morning he would do so and he felt excited thinking about it.

The next morning he dialed the number but disconnected at once. He went to his workplace and then it was like any ordinary day. He was engrossed in his daily chores which had become all the more tight owing to the accumulation of the work due to a month's strike.

The whole week passed by but he had not called her as yet. Every time he wanted to call, one thing or the other would stop him. He expressed his feelings towards me and I told him to go for it. In fact it was not a bad idea for him to move on and start a new beginning.

"May be god wants you to….Otherwise you wouldn't have been in that cab that day," I told him.

This I seriously thought. If Hari hadn't come to Sikkim, he wouldn't be travelling in that cab that day. But it was not enough. If Reema hadn't called him up he would not have had the need to use her phone and he wouldn't have talked. May be there was a reason behind her father leaving his phone behind. I told Hari that it was scripted and may be God wanted him to move on; move on yet again.

I teased him, "I think you are the only one who benefitted from the strike."

"But is this right?" He had questioned. "I mean I have been in a relationship twice and now wouldn't this be cheap again. It's just been few months that I had the last break up. And most importantly what if this too doesn't work out?"

"But it doesn't mean you should stop trying," I said, "And remember you were never the one to back out," I added lifting his spirits high.

The best love story is when you fall in love with the most unexpected person at the most unexpected time – unknown

Chapter XXXV

A Total Opposite

A week later I called him and asked, "Did you talk to her?"

"No ya, not yet, what will I tell her?"

"Come on, just call and you will know what to say."

"Ok… probably I will do it tomorrow," He said.

"Why tomorrow? Do it now," I emphasized.

"Now!…ok…but… will call up in the evening."

"Fine," I said and hung up the phone.

That evening he finally let his heart outdo his head.

"Hello?" She said.

"Hi," He said and continued, "Do you study in Loreto Convent?"

"Yes, who is this?" She inquired.

"You remember we travelled together that day from Gangtok to Darjeeling and I used your phone."

"Oh ya, I had never imagined that you would call me!" She said with overt excitement. The phone abruptly got disconnected. He was wondering what to do when she called him back.

"Sorry I had to disconnect because my father had come."

"It's okay," He said.

They had a very formal chat that day about each other's whereabouts and similar ice-breaking information. Hari also shared how awkward he had felt using her phone and how it had taken such a long time to reach Darjeeling. Most of all, he had forgotten to ask her name. She hadn't bothered too even.

He immediately narrated me their brief conversation with enthusiasm and excitement oozing out.

*

The next morning, he woke up and found a 'good morning' message from her. He had saved her number as 'The LC-ite'

Since that day Hari updated me with his progress regularly. Yet another love story was being scripted, I thought. I felt happy for him and just hoped that he succeeds this time; he really deserved to be happy. I was having a feeling that he was trying to resist. Perhaps he was too scared to fall in love again. Hari now and then kept being haunted by his past or rather his past failures and it made him feel low and erratic. Who has ever succeeded in escaping from the pain and past? It blows like a dusty wind on a beautiful autumn day.

But at the same time do we have control over our feelings. Definitely not! If it was ever possible wouldn't lives be less problematic!

By the way she was Urvashi, in her sweet seventeen. She was a Christian by faith. She was a black belt, a Taekwondo *fighter*. She had won gold at the national level and a bronze at the international level. Taekwondo is a popular sport in Darjeeling and many competitions are held all year round. Yet it does not get the proper recognition it deserves. She also played badminton and represented the school team. She loved adventure and had been trained at the Himalayan Mountaineering Institute, Darjeeling. She knew how to ride a bike and drive a car; in crux…a total opposite to him.

One thing about Urvashi was that she had always stayed away from love and relationships. But she could feel the change. She liked texting him and this she did whenever she could. Her parents had stringent rules for her. They had programmed her into thinking that she should do nothing to tarnish her career. But she was belying everyone to be in touch with him. She was confused whether she was in love or whether it was just an infatuation. On the other hand, Hari didn't just want to admit that he already had fallen for her.

Hers was a joint family. Urvashi's father was a government employee and her mother, a home maker. Her uncle worked in a bank. Her sister was in her final year of college in Delhi. Her spinster aunt worked as the Head Nurse in the Darjeeling government hospital. Talking over the phone was still difficult as she was always in company with her aunty or somebody else. She could seldom reply to those pending messages from her sweet *intruder* as she was always busy with her practices. After which she had to prepare for her board exams too.

Despite being in Darjeeling they had not yet seen each other since that fateful day.

They gradually started to talk over the phone whenever possible. She used to share her room with her aunt. But now had started to sleep alone just to be able to talk to him. And it would literally be a murmur. It was enough; they had been in touch with each other for months now and hadn't met even once. Hari finally decided that he would ask her to meet for a date.

Every heart sings a song, incomplete, until another heart whispers back. Those who wish to sing always find a song. At the touch of a lover, everyone becomes a poet – Plato

Chapter XXXVI

Candlelight Date

It was one of the Sundays of a new beginning. It was settled over the phone that they would meet in *Chowrasta* amidst the hustle and bustle of daily life. He woke up with butterflies in his stomach. He was not sure whether they would recognize each other; what her reactions would be and so many other things. At nine he reached his destination and impatiently waited for her arrival.

He looked at his watch again, it was 9:15, another fifteen minutes and she would be there, he thought. Soon it was 9:30, the stipulated time for the meet but still no signs of her. What actually made him frantic was that she had not even called him up. This meant that she was still at her home. At ten he wanted to call but chose not to. It was really difficult for her to come out alone and he wondered what reasons she might have devised to eventuate their first date. In fact, the first date of her life. She might have been more excited, he thought.

At about 10:30 she finally called him up and informed about her late arrival.

He wanted to tell her that he had been waiting for her since one and half hours but that would make her feel guilty he thought and just said,

"I can't wait to see you. Please come fast!"

Her smile which he could discern from the phone itself was enough for an answer. At eleven she finally turned up and both smiled in shyness. As their eyes met, his weariness warded off in an instance and she also forgot how tired she was feeling having rushed through a steep stairway shortcut to make up for the delay. Even the fittest of sports persons would have to catch their breath going up those stairs.

"I am so sorry I am late, actually it is because of my aunt. I hadn't told anyone that I would be coming out today, so…"

"It's ok I understand," He affirmed.

"Let's move somewhere else, I fear someone will see me with you otherwise," She said nervously, moving her head on all possible angles.

As planned the earlier night they would go around *Mall Road*. They couldn't find a place to sit down as all the view points were either occupied with other love birds or tourists busy taking pictures. So they decided to head down-town but she preferred to walk alone till the crowd got thinner. The first thing she did was to buy a few candles and a match box which made him wonder why! He got his answer as she took him to a church and made him light a candle before the statue of Jesus Christ. Then they headed towards the nearby botanical park.

Their conversation at the park was desultory and more of a monologue. Most of her answers were either in 'yes' or 'no' or either succinct. Even when he tried to look into her eyes she would just lower it avoiding any contacts. He then had a feeling that she may not have liked him. He was losing his patience but it was his first date with her so didn't want to spoil it. He had come with the intention of proposing to her but now the ambience was not as he would have liked. He still tried to make fruitful conversations but failed. He couldn't understand it was the same girl who would talk to him for long hours and sometimes till dawn and it was the same 'her' running short of words that day. Though she was calm but beneath that mask of calm exterior numerous emotions were swirling which Hari had no inkling about. He then reckoned that they go and have something but didn't get the compliance from her. Soon it was four, time to go home. Once they came out of the park she preferred to walk alone and he followed her till Chowk Bazaar. Once she reached there, she waved her hand to gesture that she was going home and with a smile she vanished amidst the narrow lanes of Chowk Bazaar. Her house Chandmari lay just half a kilometer below.

No sooner had she left, Hari's phone rang and it was her. The call made him feel immensely relieved. And it was her normal self again.

"Why didn't you respond properly in the park?" He nagged.

"Can't you understand I was really nervous and you kept looking at my eyes which made me all the more nervous."

That night they talked extensively. The night was on the verge of giving way to dawn. Hari reckoned that she must sleep as she had to go to school. But she just wouldn't agree. Their talk was finally intruded at six when her aunt called for her to wake up. She pretentiously responded as if she had just woken up from a deep sleep. They both smiled as they disconnected the call. She called him up again before she left for school. Thus, a convention got established.

He felt happy that their relationship had risen to another level. Probably they had made the right start by going to the church, he thought.

Later that night she told him how she had fallen asleep in her very first class. They both knew this was just a start of the beginning.

You know you're in love when you can't fall asleep because
reality is finally better than your dreams — Dr Suess

Chapter XXXVII

Defenseless Champ

A month lapsed and their everlasting talks skied voluminously and with it their phone bills. Hari at times felt sorry for her as she was not getting enough sleep. They would talk all night and it was always he who asked her to sleep. In the evening, she would stay till five for her Taekwondo practice. By six she would reach home. Then she would take a nap for a while and get down to her studies. This she would regularly do on the weekdays but now her timings had been intruded drastically by a stranger; a stranger whom she had felt so comfortable with in the cab; a stranger who meant quite a lot to her now. She couldn't help thinking of him even in her classes and would miss him the whole day. She couldn't wait for her school to get over. When she missed him badly she would even skip her practice. On such occasions she would surprise him with her early calls. On Hari's part he would literally count hours till her name blinked on his phone, no more as 'The LC-ite' but Urvi. Her early calls on occasions brought him extra elation.

Urvashi was feeling peculiar changes within her. All these years she had always kept away from relationships but now it seemed that she had gradually ceased to be the custodian of her own feelings; she was unable to either control or understand. However, the thought of her parents especially her aunt would make her feel cold but again her thoughts would be effortlessly driven towards her first love, Hari.

The stage was set for their next meeting. It had been an eager and impatient wait.

"Can we meet this weekend?" asked Hari.

So there he was yet again in the same *Chowrasta* waiting for his beloved and as usual she was hyper late and he, hyper early! The previous evening, they had planned to walk to Jorebunglow, a renowned landmark, and then an hour's walk uphill would lead them to the famous 'Tiger Hill'.

She finally came and *thank God!* She was late only by an hour this time. They strolled across *Chowrasta* with Hari following her. Having walked a few yards alone, a sudden thought passed her mind and she stopped.

"Let's walk together," She said. She must have realized that they couldn't live this way forever.

"Are you sure?" He cross-checked. She just nodded in reply and the nod made him feel like a king.

They decided to walk through the *Alubari* road which was comparatively empty. It was her idea to walk that route and now he understood why. He felt like holding her hand as they walked but knowing the kind of person she was, it would be utterly indecent, he thought. That day she was a bit composed though and responded properly which made him happy. As they strolled along the solitary *Alubari* road, her talks revolved around her school, her practices and most importantly her two friends Divya and Sandra.

In between such casual conversations Hari asked,

"What will you do after your 12?"

"Mmmm... I want to join a nursing institute."

"Seriously?"

"Ya! What's wrong with that?"

"Nothing, but I was thinking that you are more into sports and adventure."

"Ya sports is my passion."

"But don't you think it's cool to make your passion a profession. The best part is you get paid for the thing you love doing."

"Ya even my parents say that but for me passion and profession are different. More so sports in the hills do not have a future."

For them it was their 'walk to remember' though nothing *fancy* happened. After about an hour's walk they finally reached Jorebunglow.

"Now what?" She asked Hari.

"Let's have something and then we will move towards the Tiger Hill," Said Hari.

"Let's do one thing, we will buy edibles and then walk as we might get late," She reckoned, to which Hari readily agreed.

With every passing minute she was feeling cozier and more comfortable. After walking uphill for a while they reached a certain place where cemented benches were raised for the passersby to repose. They decided to rest for a while munching the things they had brought.

The wind was cold but not draughty. The blue sky above was dappled with fleecy clouds making the spectacle splendid. The chilly wind would now and again kiss her dimpled cheeks replenishing them with profuse pinkness just like the first blossoms of cherry. Hari was capturing the very moment in the lens of his mind.

They spent quite a deal of time and now they were sitting close by. Urvashi had brought her digital camera. She introduced him to her family members stating who was who and at what instance those snaps were taken, a universal way of pictoral introduction. After she completed hers, it was Hari's turn to repeat the same procedure, which he performed from the phone itself. As he browsed his picture gallery, she moved a little closer giving him the same feeling he had had that day in the cab. It was as if the closeness was being replicated.

As she was engrossed in his pictures and his selfies, he minutely scanned her dreamy eyes, her untamed eyebrows, her steadily *pinking* cheeks, her fitting nose and her beautiful lips. He didn't know what happened to him; he leaned towards her and in the next spur-of-the-moment kissed her on the lips. The taekwondo champ was rendered defenseless. She abruptly withdrew and gasped for air as she freed herself from his mouth. She got up, zipped her jumper to the neck.

She quietly slipped to a nearby bench, sat there with firmly folded hands and her back towards him. Probably she hadn't expected this in her wildest dreams. She remained glued in contemplation.

Hari didn't know what to do and chose to wait for her response. Few moments later, she came back and acted as if nothing had happened. Hari presumed that she wanted to forget the kiss and move on. But he wouldn't just let her go today, he was determined. He kissed her again and yet again. She withdrew after a while and then proclaimed that she was getting late. Both of them were excited enough. For Hari it was a new beginning and for the girl the beginning itself was new. Hari decided to make a proposal to her, whether she accepts or not was not a million dollar question now. Still Hari was nervous as was she. With some courage he put forward his proposition of love to her; he constantly felt the rate of his heartbeat burgeoning.

He said, "I kissed you only because I love you. I really love you a lot and I realized I fell for you when I met you for the first time when you sat beside me. Then as you fiddled with your phone I felt jealous thinking that you were texting your boyfriend. I felt so complete when you sat close to me and void as you left. That day itself I wanted to hold your hand but couldn't muster up the courage. But now I can say that I love you. Will you be my girlfriend?" He proposed at last.

On the other hand the receiver stood silently with coyness, bended her brows and simply smiled. She pondered over his words, but said nothing. She didn't reply and he didn't ask for it again. He could not understand clearly the gestures that she was making nevertheless he felt happy for being able to open out his heart to her. In another half an hour they headed towards their own paths; without completely understanding the emotion that they shared for each other in such a short span of time.

Later that night they talked as usual but unusually Urvashi asked Hari if he could meet her the very next day. "Are you serious?" He asked with astonishment.

> *The heart doesn't need reason to fall in love but*
> *its love that needs reason to find the heart*

Chapter XXXVIII

Dum and Drunk

Around 11 am the long awaited moment finally arrived. Both of them after their respective duties of different kind decided to meet at the same place where they had met for the first time. Still in her utmost coyness, she stared at the ground and asked Hari,

"Do you really love me?"

"Yes," He replied without really thinking deep, and in haste he asked,

"What makes you think I don't?"

"Nothing! Was just thinking about our last meet the whole night; I couldn't even sleep."

"You got to trust me."

"Yes, I do. But when I think of what happened to my aunt, I get scared," She said in a rehearsed manner.

"Why? What happened to her?"

"Papa often tells me her story of how she had fallen in love with some man and he had promised her of marriage.

Unfortunately that man left my aunt for some other woman. How sad she must have been then!"

"I can understand the pain in love vividly. And yes, I assure you that I am serious about what I told you yesterday."

Urvashi looked at his face for a while and out of the blue, embraced him with warmth. He at once knew that it was her arms wherein he could bring the child in him out, let it grow and pass away. At that moment he was thinking if there's heaven on earth, it was right there and at that very moment; in her arms.

After a prolonged contemplation she said, "Yesterday you told me how you felt when you sat close to me in that cab. That day I too felt something which I will tell you today. When you asked me for my phone to use, I wanted your number too. I don't know whether I would make a call to you or not but I did want your number and that is the reason why I asked for it to transfer the balance." That way I would have had it."

Hari was surprised but was very happy to understand that love had really been at the first sight.

Urvashi went on, "I felt so at home and cozy with you in that cab and so I didn't shift a bit though you were so close to me and sometimes even our hands would touch each other's. I loved each and every touch that day. And when you left I felt so void, incomplete and detached. I looked at you and was sure that I would never see you again. This thought hurt me that night. You were a stranger then but I felt that I have always known you. And when you called me I felt so very happy and excited. That day I felt that the thing called soul mates do exist and I feel that we are soul mates."

Hari was quick to interrupt, "Yes soul mates...that is what we exactly are. I will give you a book to read and it's called Brida."

"A book!... That would be nice," Said Urvashi and continued, "But I always wanted to be away from love and relationship and I have reasons. I think of my family, my aunty and so many other things. I don't even know if I am doing an appropriate thing or not. I also feel that I can't give you much time, dedication and love you deserve."

To this Hari replied, "Whatever you can afford, will be enough for me," She gazed at him with eyes replete with love.

That day they promised many things which were like fairy tales and Hari was aware of it. But not to disturb her he went on with one commitment to another. And when they finally parted, both were flying high with the wings of love without having knowledge of what was in store for them next.

Later they went to the market and Hari bought a diary for her which she would keep with her unwritten, probably she would keep all her feelings and Hari tucked away safe in her heart. The diary would be her prized possession. She bestowed Hari with a huge packet of chocolates. He smiled as he opened the packet. It took him to the old times as he remembered how he longed for chocolates then. He felt like a child as he had it.

Before they departed he was taken to one of the famous places of Darjeeling. No, not a tourist spot or anywhere posh but what is famously known as *'Bari Ko Dokan'*, a small and shabby canteen owned by an elderly lady whom everyone addresses as *'bari'*, meaning aunt. This canteen is famous for *'alu dum'*, potato gravy. Many believe she sells the best *alu dum*.

The people of Darjeeling love potatoes it seems, and the favourite dish out here inarguably has to be *alu dum*. My god, these people have improvised quite a variety out of the simple *alu dum* – *alu bhuja*, *alu mix*, *alu mimi*, *alu cheese balls*, and to take it further, these come in two categories – special or plain. And you get it in every nook and corners of Darjeeling.

'Bari Ko Dokan' is popular especially among the women folk but some guys also turn up to get a taste of Bari's delicacy. And like Urvashi many of the girlfriends would invariably bring their boyfriends too.

The canteen is very small and only few people can fit in. So many are found outside the shop gulping the delicacy in a standing-point; unable to have the patience to wait. However, that day few seats were vacant and she ushered him inside. *Bari*, an old woman with distorted teeth immediately recognized her and forwarded her two plates of *alu dum*. Urvashi at once gobbled it up and asked for another one. Hari tasted and found it spicy and thought that the taste of *Bari's alu dum* was simply eulogized and wondered why people made it such a hub. But he kept this thought to himself so as not to offend her. She asked whether he wanted more to which he declined and opted to have *momo* instead. He found *momo* tastier and asked for another plate while she still opted for the 'heartthrob dish'. Both feeling satisfied finally abdicated their place for those waiting in queue.

Small shops like this are popular among the lovers in Darjeeling as these places bring them together without any space literally.

*

Their next date was totally unexpected. He had gone to his friends' wedding and was drunk. I still remember the day February 24, 2010. In Gwalior, cricketing history had been created and it had taken 2,961 games. Sachin had made the first ever double century in the ODIs and it was against the South Africans. And the commentator Ravi Shastri had immaculately encapsulated the moment as...

"It is the superman from India who has done it," And yes he was right when he said that Sachin had used his blade (bat) like a surgeon's knife.

Hari messaged as he was returning, "Hey I am drunk, hyper drunk."

She called him and asked, "Can you meet me today?"

"But I am not at all in a condition to meet," He objected.

"I want to," She insisted.

"Please understand," He pleaded.

"I am alone. Meet me if you love me," She said and disconnected the phone.

Later he would know why she had forced him to meet. She had never seen him in a drunken state and had called him only to see the spectacle.

Hari was conscious enough to walk and act with composure but his intoxicated legs would not entail him to do so. They slowly walked towards *Lal Kothi*, another landmark considered to be one of the finest residential addresses in Bengal during its pristine glory, half a century ago. It had been a beautiful day and as the love birds moved in cozy pace, hand-crossed, the still treetops basked in the evening rays. As they walked on the solitary road they could see the colonial cottages so beautifully and proudly keeping their stand firm. It looked all the more beautiful as the evening rays pierced through the pine trees and shone on the cottages.

The tall pine trees on either side would sometimes allow the penetrating chilly wind to brush Hari's cheeks aiding to deescalate his drunkenness. Rhododendrons and camellias had blossomed in competition all along the breezy boulevard of February. They walked on. Probably, he didn't realize but his actions, especially his stumbling stalks would make her laugh which she was doing innately, enjoying it enormously. After all, her motive was accomplished and whenever she thought of it, it would endow her face with a smile.

> *I don't know what you have that I can't help*
> *falling in love with you. But I guess what you have*
> *is just what I wanted and all that I needed*

Chapter XXXIX

Caught

It had been a few months since they had started seeing each other but their closeness felt ages old. They would talk about their past, their present and their future. Now they seemed so committed that they had even laid a *future* blueprint. Even the names of their children were decided. Hari would sometimes tease her saying that she must be the first from her school at least who was thinking of marriage and things like that.

Urvashi on her part never let her busy schedule encroach upon their everlasting talks. The huge *cleavage* in age between the two meant nothing. They seemed to have realized that it was just love that was needed for a relationship to work. However, there was one thing which bothered them a bit and that was their respective religious faiths. Hari was of the opinion that they would keep their respective beliefs and would respect each other's faith. But how far it was practically feasible he wasn't sure of. After all he didn't know how their respective parents would react. He thought his parents would comply without much fuss.

Bipin Baral

But for Urvashi things were different. She was too young, a high school girl and in a career-building phase. It was not the right time to break the news to her parents. Hari thought that he would wait for the right opportunity. Innately he knew that everything will work out as they had planned. It is just a matter of time, he thought. They could elope if they really wanted to be together but this conservative girl would not comply with it, he knew it.

*

In one of their dates they decided to go to Siliguri and spend their day there. Urvashi lied to her parents that she would be going with Divya and Sandra. Everything was taken care of so that they wouldn't be caught. The *Rohini* road on the way to Siliguri is exotic and if the weather is clear the view is just splendid. But the road is very narrow and there is hardly any room for two vehicles to pass by simultaneously. On one of the turnings their vehicle got stuck by a private car which was on its way to Darjeeling. Urvashi and Hari were on the front seat and she was resting her head on Hari's left shoulder. Suddenly, Urvashi moved away and nervously looked down trying to cover her face. Hari couldn't figure out what happened. She muttered, "My relatives are in that car!"

She got caught. Her family had been noticing the changes in her and now their ever growing suspicion was confirmed.

"Are you nuts, he is much older to you… you understand what it means?" Her mother scolded.

Her sister professed, "Your thoughts won't match in the long run, so it's better that you end it right now when it's not too late. If you go deep then it will be tough for you," She would add, "It's just an infatuation. It happens in teenage, you can get over it."

The news of her affair proliferated to the other members of her house and it led to a great debate amongst them. There were three primary hurdles. The first being the huge age gap between the two; second being her board exams and her taekwondo career and most importantly their religion.

Her aunt especially had asked her, "Will he be able to convert to Christianity for you?"

Love is never without complications and hurdles. In fact, it is the trials that give it a meaning and charm. It is the will and ability to tackle these problems that gives us wisdom; wisdom to love and wisdom to live.

After the cat was out of the bag, Urvashi had to be the object of sarcasm and ridicule at times. All of a sudden she was the focus and everyone at home seemed to be extra watchful of her. Urvashi however was determined not to let this affect their relationship. But how long could she? After all there is a limit to everything. Her family members soon found out that she was still in touch with him and this time they asked her to make a choice between her family and Hari.

In fact, they were also not totally wrong. After all, they loved her more. She was young and needed to be protected and one wrong step from her would tarnish her family's name but her studies and career too. She may have found the right person but who at her age knew what was right and what was not. How could her parents believe that their teenage daughter had found a prince charming and they were going to live happily ever after!

She contemplated on many possibilities the whole week. She had been hiding her pain and her sufferings from him but now she needed an outlet. He had to be told face to face what she was facing rather than confide over the phone.

I can't promise to fix all your problems but I can promise you won't have to face them alone —Unknown

Chapter XL

Homeless

There he was yet again waiting for her at the old destination. As usual he was early but unusually she was punctual today.

Before meeting her, Hari went to the nearby stores and desperately searched for something good to gift her. Finally after a laborious search he found three items which ignited his interest; a black Puma sweater, a purple sweater and the pink jumper. He had already paid for the first one when his eyes caught sight of another one in purple the mannequin was wearing. He then imagined her in it; it would just look superb on her; he bought that too without a second thought. Just then his eyes caught hold of another jumper. He imagined her in it. He ended up buying that too. This he would keep hidden in his back-pack and would give it to her only before they *departed* for *home*.

He saw her approaching and noticed that she was carrying her Tiffin box in one hand and an umbrella on the other. As usual her hair was carelessly tied and her face was devoid of chemicals. She was looking beautiful in her pink windcheater. That day she wanted to take a joy ride in the famous toy train of Darjeeling. As they approached Jorebunglow they got down from the running train. Perhaps it is the only train in the world where you don't need a stoppage to get down. You can even get down from the running train, buy flowers for your beloved and get into it with ease.

They headed towards Tiger Hill and as usual went to a corner which they had patronized as 'their' spot. From there one could see a superb panorama of mount Kanchenjunga with Darjeeling town in the foreground nestled between the majestic pine trees and the ever so famous tea gardens.

She handed the Tiffin box to him and boasted, "Your breakfast, *alu parantha,* your favourite... I made it," Though he was not feeling hungry he had it with pride.

Finally the moment of truth had come and she was all set to tell him what he ought to know. She still in his arms; with her head resting on his chest said,

"My parents have found out between you and me and they created a commotion. Not only that now everyone snares at me and even my aunty has stopped talking to me properly. They say that we can't be together and even our religion doesn't permit. I don't think our relation will work and I think we should end it once and for all," She uttered the last line with a heavy breath.

Hari's face grew solemn.

He became ruminative and after a while said, "I knew they would create problems and I don't blame them for it. We have to admit that there are many complications between us including our age gap. But we just need to carry on for three years or so and everything will be normal. By then I will also get settled and you too would have completed your college. So it's just a matter of time, we need to take it slow," He suggested conclusively.

She shook her head in negation and said, "You don't understand my predicament. Every day, every time, I have to face their sarcasm and their snares. I can't take it any minute further and you are talking about years. And moreover they have asked me to choose between you and them. And don't think that it's easy for me. I know what I am about to lose. You are the best part of me remember that. But I can't go against my parents."

He felt an overarching pain. His life which had gradually begun to settle down suddenly became topsy-turvy again! He tried to make her understand but she wouldn't even try to ponder upon his suggestions. He had no option left so he said, "It's ok then," He gasped looking towards the misty mountains and said, "Since you have decided it; I can't say anything and can't force. Ok, we will end whatever is there between us right now and from this very moment but please accept this."

He handed her the gifts which he had bought for her. She accepted it hesitatingly. They now headed towards their ways in different directions. With her he had felt so much at home, but now that she was gone, he felt homeless.

Later that night she messaged him, "I am sorry but I hope you understand."

He replied, "Yes dear I will understand, I have always understood. As you know I am used to departures. But please don't ever doubt my love towards you. Know that I have always tried to give you the best of my love, dedication, care, concern and trust. I don't know how much of it you felt but from my side I did try. Having said that I have to thank you for all the things you have given me. Thank you for being my better half, my girl friend for little over a 100 days. Thank you for all the troubles you took just to talk to me or be with me. Thank you for everything. I have thoroughly enjoyed your presence and I will remember it for a long, long time." He sent it and started typing again.

"And I am sorry for all the times that I have hurt you or not lived up to your expectations. But most importantly I am sorry, so sorry for touching you inappropriately. But believe me I never ever thought for that moment only. All the improper things that I could do were just because I love you and always thought that I would see the end with you. Had really planned my future with you and that's why I was always telling you so many things that I would do later on for you (like taking you to river side quite often, Paragliding; remember we were supposed to have an attic?; you had agreed to wash my clothes always and I would be preparing you delicacies on weekends…and so many other things)… So it didn't even occur to me that I was doing improper things to you. But now I am seriously and sincerely sorry ok!

Just one thing more, I felt love when we touched each other for the first time and I feel love even as I bid you good bye. Just stay happy always and take immense care… pray that your days after 'me' be the happiest days of your life… take care."

She replied, "How I wish you could read my heart...just know that I can survive but I can't really live without you."

Hari chose not to reply.

But deep down he felt that all was not lost. He hoped that things would get normal and that she would eventually come back. But the long days passed by and the longer nights await. Maybe she doesn't need him now the way he needs her, he would think. But he would find himself falling...falling deeper...deeper into the pit.

He would hold his phone for a call but the next moment he would think, 'it is not right'. He would end up holding it and crying at the screen. Every message, every call he received in his phone, he would think it to be hers and especially those that beeped at nights. He would wake up hurriedly to check his phone, only to get disappointed.

*

One night he checked his *Whatsapp* and viewed her profile. She had updated her status, "I am letting the best part of me go away." Then he realized that it was all over.

He never discerned that his romantic cameo with her would end in such an abrupt way. As he went to bed, he found himself reverted to the old perpetual loneliness where he would gaze at the unbothered ceiling in contemplation of the bygone times.

I miss you even more than I could have believed; and I was prepared to miss you a good deal — Vita Sackville-West

Chapter XLI

Chowrasta

Time isn't always the best healer; sometimes it's just that we get subsumed by it.

Hari was feeling very lonely and void. It had been more than a week that he had not been in touch with her. He took a day off and decided to spend his day alone at his favorite hangout in Darjeeling, the *Chowrasta*; sit there and hope to see her. The weather that day was as misty and cold as Hari's heart. He was missing something dreadfully in his life. Was it love again that was something he wanted to adorn or was it, its experience he wanted to cherish. The howling wind at *Chowrasta* shook his soul. He felt cold and dejected. The ache was something he knew well, but the void this time was just colossal.

It had started drizzling and every pour of the rain reminded him of his misfortune. He chose to get wet hoping the chilly rain would console his despair. Hari was the lonely soul at the *Chowrasta* bench, and without an umbrella, as the frosty rain slowly drenched him from head to toe. Just then an old lady came and sat near him. She generously gestured to share her umbrella but he declined the offer and chose to *painjoy* the drizzle. As the downpour increased, Hari had a feeling that the rain was trying to drench his pain out. It stopped abruptly and the sun had come out again. Hari felt strange and looked at the grandma in an apologetic manner. She just smiled, and said "Life is how you decide to live, in the rain or not in the rain but someone else decides if you should be in the rain or you shouldn't… and for how long. See, the sun has already come now." Hari was awestruck by the elderly lady's explanation. He took it to his mind.

Chowrasta restored its typicality, bustling with life once again; with people walking around, children playing, and the dogs and pigeons back to their hangout. The malnourished horses were now out of their stables and compelled to charm their owners more than the tourists. Perhaps these creatures believe and are grateful that they are fed and cared for by their owners. Little do they know that it's the other way round!

Darjeeling, normally designated as the 'Queen of Hills' probably is one of the best places on earth to be in. The roads are very narrow and many parts of it are in a way mucky. In the contemporary Darjeeling, the notion of development boils down to the mushrooming of concrete structures in place of the colonial ones, a stark testimony of 'unplanned planning'. Yet Darjeeling has this old-world charm and a peculiar aura, and of course, its idiosyncrasies – attracting thousands of tourists each year.

And of the many tourist destinations, *Chowrasta* endeavours to stand *tall* amidst the rush of material modernity, indeed a unique place to be in. Situated at the top of the town it is probably the most visited place especially among the locals. During my many stays in *Chowrasta*, I have repeatedly heard the locals declaring that they feel incomplete without visiting and being there even for a while, whenever they are out. I have not been able to discern the reasons as to what makes the place so loved. Whatever the reasons are, people just flock to this place. However, the most peculiar aspect of it is that you can sit for hours at a stretch without even getting bored. Being there with friends will just spice up the sojourn. I have always felt that *Chowrasta* is an epitome of Darjeeling and also its heart. Being there will fairly orient you with the people of Darjeeling; their perceptions and their outlooks. There's so much of activity taking place in *Chowrasta* which would not be hard for an onlooker to observe.

Horse riding is one of the major activities there. Hari witnessed the activities of the horse owners trying to coax the tourists for a ride. At one end Hari witnessed a group of tourists being pestered by the horsemen to choose their horses for a ride. Three horses were chosen; two however had to wait for other tourists. Just then a group of giggling girls passed by.

My God! The Darjeeling girls are really beautiful. And I always had a feeling that god created them at leisure, may be on Sundays! Their reddish skin, their mesmerizing look and their immaculate dressing sense make them uniquely different. They definitely enrich the splendor of this majestic abode.

Hari was feeling lonely; it had been days since he last heard her voice. He was hoping that he would at least get a glimpse of her. But he was not sure what he would do if he happened to see her.

Hari resumed his contemplation; he remembered how she used to put him in awkward situations. He remembered being made to say those three magical words 'I Love You' while he would be travelling in cabs, in full audience of the co-passengers. She would ask, "Is there a girl sitting next to you?" All was over. Off late he travelled without those awkward queries. She loved entrapping him and he loved being entrapped. He remembered how she would make him sing out loud at midnight and how he would have to narrate stories to lullaby her to sleep. Then he had a feeling that he would have sung right there in the midst of *Chowrasta...* tell her thousands of stories just to conquer her back. He would have done anything to get the love of his life back.

With these swirling thoughts in mind he found himself sitting in one of the freshly painted benches there; the only public welfare performed by the municipality in Darjeeling. The benches in *Chowrasta* are very old and at the outset one would feel that there is nothing fascinating about it. However, the enigmatic beauty of the place itself is hard to decode. He wanted to occupy one among the particular row of benches there, as he knew her frequently travelled route, but it was occupied already. So he situated himself in one of the vacant seats on the other side. His bench was soon intruded by a young couple. The guy seemed to be despondent for reasons unknown to Hari. Soon he found out. The girl presumably had done something wrong and she was repeatedly apologizing in a very childish yet in a sweet manner.

Then how he wished that his love too had done the same; his world would be alive again. However, he couldn't help himself from eavesdropping though it was improper. Some of their talks were bringing a faint smile to his face, which he couldn't hide. On another day it probably would not have mattered to him much and their talks would just mean nothing to him, but today was not any other day. Their talks made him discern that they had had a breakup the previous night, but somehow today they met. The guy was from Mirik, the sub-division from where Kavita hailed.

On the other side there were a group of middle aged people gossiping. One among them regretted - how back in 1970s, he had missed the rare opportunity to buy a strategically located land with plentitude of water resources. Water supply in Darjeeling is quite erratic. I remember one of my friends who always used to tell me when I stayed at his place, "Please use water rationally." People of Darjeeling are very open hearted but when it comes to water they are the meanest and hard core misers.

The sudden barking of dogs galvanized Hari from his engrossment. A rag picker was having a tough time getting rid of the dogs. These dogs are among the permanent dwellers of *Chowrasta*. It is only when the yearly 'Dog Show' is held and the clean sophisticated dogs intrude their haven; these permanent dwellers take refuge to the *Mall Road* and nearby places. Even the dogs feel inferiority complex, it seems. The old man was still finding it hard to rescue himself from the dogs. Hari witnessed it for a while, when his vision was blocked by a man who was walking his motor bike through the middle of *Chowrasta*. From the other end a lady strolled with her baby in the perambulator.

Love seems to be in the air in Darjeeling and *Chowrasta* is not an exception. All generations young to old seem to find love in Darjeeling. These lovers walk hand in hand with the one who means the world to them, though only a few would make it to the end. Hari was feeling jealous at times making him feel sordidly lonely. He was missing his Urvi so much and the fact she was gone would choke him innately. He thought of calling her up surpassing everything. He just wanted to forget for a while that it was she who had bowed down to the hindrances. This made his heart all the more heavy but he was not enraged; he was just feeling empty. Every thought of her would aggravate his pain and compound to his perpetual loneliness.

After a while some people from the other bench left, he shifted there. This was a strategic place for him as far as his chance of seeing her was concerned. From there he could patrol three sides. He was literally looking at every girl hoping that it was her. He wanted to see just one face in the entire Darjeeling; the face of his life, Urvashi.

He missed being with her. He missed the smell of her perfume. He missed her never ending talks about petty issues. He missed everything she did. Then he had flashbacks about the times he would come to meet her. He missed their dates at Tiger Hill and of course his first kiss to her;

the first kiss of her life. He remembered telling her in the evening over the phone that he felt like he was kissing a stone or a log; but it had in a way felt sensuous, innocent and charming. In fact it was that imperfect act of hers that made it all the more special; it was far better than thousand perfect smooches, he had let her know. It was an emotional endeavor from her side. But the only emotion she felt was of fear. If truth be told their love story had begun after that particular kiss. The stringent fluttering of the *Chowrasta* pigeons brought him back to reality. He didn't realize that a guy next to him had been replaced by an old man who was slurping his tea. He must have spent a good deal of time, he thought and smiled.

I think part of the reason why we hold on to
something so tight is because we fear something
so great won't happen twice – Unknown

Chapter XLII

The Ultimate Truth

18 September, 2011. Himalayan earthquake had hit Sikkim with a magnitude of 6.9 and was centered within the Kanchenjunga Conservation Area, near the border of Nepal and Sikkim. It was just two days before that Hari had gone to Delhi for his office chores. However, the disturbing news made Hari return to his hometown earlier than stipulated.

Hari had just boarded the train when he received a call from an unknown number.

"Hello," He said.

"Is this Hari?" The voice on the other side inquired.

"Yes what is it?" He said.

"This is Inspector Rakesh from Darjeeling Sadar Police station. You are to visit the police station at the earliest."

"Why? What's the matter?" He asked anxiously.

"You come over, we will discuss the matter then," The inspector said refusing to divulge further detail.

"But… I am in Delhi and have just started," He sighed. "Hopefully I will reach Siliguri tomorrow," He quickly added.

"Anyway just come straight over as and when you reach," The inspector proclaimed, adding, "It's about Urvashi."

A sudden chill sprinted inside Hari from head to toe, the conversation ended with a few 'Hellos' from the other side. Hari was worried what she might have done to get entangled with the Law. He dialed her number instantly but found it switched off. During the entire journey he was preoccupied with her thoughts and it made him immensely worried. He tried to think of other sources but he couldn't. It made him panicky.

Unable to curtail his anxiety he called me up and briefed me about his talk with the inspector. He further asked, "Man, can you go to Darjeeling early tomorrow?"

"Ya I will but I won't be able to go very early as I have errands of my own which in no way I can evade," I said. I was confused and worried at the same time.

"Don't worry! I promise I will definitely go at the earliest and find out everything I can," I assured.

Next day I boarded a shared taxi to Darjeeling at 10 am. Meanwhile Hari kept on calling me; I could understand how frantic and worried he was. I reached the Darjeeling police station at 2 in the afternoon and inquired for Inspector Rakesh. I was directed to his chamber by a constable. "Hello sir," I greeted and introduced myself as Hari's friend and also made him learn where I had come from.

"Hari is on his way and he will be reaching today. He was really worried so he asked me to be acquainted with the matter," I explained.

The inspector briefed me about the incident and I couldn't believe what my ears had just heard.

"When did it happen?" I asked in desperation.

"Yesterday morning," He bluntly said.

"Oh!" I sighed.

"What does the post-mortem report reveal?" I inquired further.

"It seems there is no foul play; it was her own doing."

"She had left a suicide note and it is designated to him. We had some inquiries to make," He added at once.

"Can I see the note?" I said in an impulse.

"Actually we don't allow but… just have a glance."

I felt a vicarious pain after I read the letter. I was moved at what she had written. I handed the letter back to the inspector.

At that very moment Hari called me up and I didn't know what to do. I looked at Rakesh who gestured me not to tell anything. I nodded in affirmation and sneaked outside.

"I have reached but inspector Rakesh is not here. I have been informed that he will be here any time," I said.

"Ok then be there and do inform me as soon as you get to know anything. I have reached Siliguri and will take at the most three hours," He hung up.

*

At five the dreaded moment finally arrived. I went out to receive him. I tried to maintain a face of composure. As I approached him I informed that the inspector had just arrived and was waiting for him. I promptly directed him to the inspector's chamber. The inspector after a quick handshake asked Hari to take a seat. He immediately handed him the letter. My heart raced as he opened the letter and it raced further as he started to read it. As he read he grew sullen.

She had written…

"Beloved Hari,

I thought and thought and have finally come to this. I really love you a lot and can't do without you. I waited for things to get back to normal but now I know that it never will. I am in such a dilemma that I can't live without you and nor can I betray my parents. So I choose to end myself.

But I want you to carry on with your dreams and all those things we have dreamt of. I know you are a fighter and won't give up. Like you have risen bravely earlier, this time too I want you to rise as you have never before. Remember, every tear you shed will hurt me and every wrong step you take will shatter me. I didn't have a choice but you have.

Please forgive me that I am leaving you like this. You will be shattered I know. I had promised to be there with you forever but I guess I have lived my share of life and I am thankful that before I had to leave, I met you. But know that I am always there with you in your happiness, in your joys and sorrows and in your heart.

I have always felt so happy and complete with you. I thought that it will pass by and I will get over you but then I thought getting over you will be like getting over myself and it will be injustice to all the unflinching love, the unconditional cares, and trust you have bestowed upon me. Thank you for all. I know you will never forget me, but I want you to move on. You have so many dreams and every dream you fulfill, will be a testimony that you still love me the way you have always done.

I also want you to look for a nice girl and get married. I feel jealous when I say this but like you have taught me, love conquers it all. I love you so much and if there is any afterlife and rebirth, I will definitely be yours and won't let you go."

He stood aghast holding the edge of the table. He was experiencing his own quake, only that its magnitude couldn't be measured. He stared at me but I couldn't look into his eyes. I just draped my hand tenderly across his shoulder. He broke down. The inspector offered him a glass of water. After a few moments when Hari calmed a bit, the inspector started the inquiry replete with probing questions.

"I want to see her for the last time," He said and in the next moment we were heading towards her home, the direction of which we didn't know precisely. It had become murky by the time we had come out of the station. Hari did know that she lived in Chandmari. Moreover, it wouldn't be difficult to find her house as the news would have well disseminated by now.

We navigated our way to her house. It got dark by the time we reached. It was a beautiful cottage surrounded by a lovely flower garden. There were quite a number of people in the house. I knew I would have to take charge from here and so I asked a lady whether we could meet any relatives of Urvashi. The lady told us to be seated while she would fetch somebody. On her way she asked a young girl to bring tea for us. We waited on a settee.

After a while she came with Urvashi's father. Hari immediately recognized him and greeted him with "*Namaste*," The man greeted him back but he didn't recognize Hari.

"I am Hari," He said with a rueful smile and there was a moment of silence after that. I could discern signs of repentance in the unfortunate father's face.

He asked us to excuse him and went inside directing us to have our tea and snacks laid in front of us. I sipped few sips of tea while Hari chose to have nothing. The man came with few other people and in the next moment we found ourselves in the midst of her relatives. At that moment a thought struck me. Probably Hari might have wanted to be there amidst her family asking for her hand in marriage but today he was there to ask them to see her face for the very last time.

Hari with composure asked, "Can I see her for the last time?"

One among them revealed, "Her funeral is already done."

He lurched back into the chair.

He couldn't control it anymore and cried in agony, "I couldn't even see her for the last time!"

To this her father moved forward and took him in his arms. This sight brought tears in the eyes of the other members of the family. Some cried discreetly, and others openly.

Some normalcy restored a while later and Hari out of the blue asked in a faltering tone, "Can I see her room?"

I didn't know why he wanted to see it. Nevertheless, her family members directed us to her room. Hari knew the room very well. She had already described him about the nitty-gritty of the room numerous times. We entered the room. It was quite spacious and at the entrance there lay a photo frame of her; she had been deduced to just a frame.

He looked at her bed; it was the same place from where she talked to him for long hours. He kneeled down on the floor near her bed and hugged it as if she was still sleeping there. He could in fact smell the faint reminiscence of her body fragrance; it hurt him all the more. He got up in a stagger and without seeking any permission, opened her wardrobe. He knew the contents of the wardrobe so very well. He reached out to a certain part of the wardrobe and took out something as if it was his own. It was a diary containing a few scribbles in her handwriting. She had diligently hidden it. His eyes met with few lines and he immediately knew those were meant for him. She had scribbled childishly.

Who has seen the façade of time?
Who has seen tomorrow!
It's unknown, uncertain and unpredictable
What if I close my eyes tomorrow?
And forever would sleep on my bed
How would you know then?
How much you are loved
And how dear you are to me
Until unspoken words are gifted to you
May be you'll find another
Who would rain down the stars for you!
But though in a small corner of that heart
I'll be there, still loving you and making you realize
That I was true and my love for you was real, not fake!

Hari was experiencing a plethora of emotions within. I was in two minds, whether to console him or let him live his lifeless moments; those 'unknown', 'uncertain' and 'unpredictable'.

That night we stayed at her place. In the morning I got up to find that Hari was not there. I went outside and enquired. I was told that he had gone to the cemetery. It was just a few yards below her house. He was near her epitaph bending on his knees. How difficult it must have been for him to see the love of his life nailed into the coffin and buried to the ground. To me he appeared like a vanquished soldier in the battle of life.

Six feet under she lay prostrate, motionless and lifeless and six feet above Hari knelt motionless and lifeless. All their hopes, their dreams, their desires buried well beneath the rubble. All distances can be covered in this world but this was just irrecoverable.

He had lost it all; the love of his life; his faith, his zest and his will to carry on. It was too difficult for him to bear with the irreversible loss this time. He had always been an optimist thinking that whatever happened will at least be beneficial and good for the one who left. But this time he couldn't console himself. He could find neither words nor reasons.

People say love is an epitome of God, but the same God in the form of religion had taken away his love. The societal norms came as great barriers which deconstructed his life and dragged him back to the same point from where he had started. Look at the irony of Hari's fate. All the years he yearned for true love and when he had found one it began to fade as quickly as it had appeared. Fate had always been harsh on him but cruel this time.

Times have changed and we proclaim that we live in a modern society. However, few absurd social constructs are still so deeply embedded and rampant in our society. Religion has led to wars but it also had led to such a thing which Hari had to witness. People still don't understand that after all we are worshipping one Supreme Being called

God, though we have different names for it. I remember my granny's saying – religions are all but rivers leading us to an ocean called God. She is so right.

Life is precious and disturbances in any form should not be allowed to end it. Traditions and cultures are definitely important but still not as important as life itself, after all life is created but traditions are only made.

I believe love is never complete without hurdles and complications. In fact, it is the trials that give it a meaning and charm. It is the will and ability to tackle these problems that gives us wisdom; wisdom to love and wisdom to live.

Life is precious and living supreme and we should learn to live rather than ending it. After all we just have one life to live and eternal silence after that.

That night he wrote in his diary:

"Why did you have to do this? I hate you for it and I will not be able to forgive myself for killing you as it was my love that made you do this. I regret being there in that cab that day. How I wish I hadn't felt love when I touched you and how I wish you didn't feel the same. How I wish I hadn't called you, you would be alive. You wouldn't be mine but at least you would still be here. You are forever mine but still I remain a loser. What's the essence in this when I can't see you nor hear you or touch you! How can I mend this love that has left me so incomplete that whatever I do I succumb to this empty space. Your stillness has consumed me like wildfire. Our love has lost and without you, 'your fighter' can't wield his sword anymore...

I lost myself in the process of losing you."

> *Life speaks so much of us but death doesn't*
> *have to, its silence is enough for all*

Chapter XLIII

Distant Rehab

Everyone will meet with the ultimate truth at one point of time or the other but for Hari, she went away rather quickly. May be he thought if she was a bit matured, she wouldn't have done what she did but now he could only think of million 'ifs' and 'buts' which eventually would make no difference. She was gone forever, only his congealed wound remained.

It was enough for him; he wouldn't be able to take it anymore. I felt guilty in a way that it was on my insistence that he had been close to her, I thought. I tried talking sense to him but it was futile. There was no way out and what words could I create to make him understand if not lessen his pain. The catastrophe was corroding him from within. He felt void and daunted thinking of his life ahead without her.

*

One evening Hari called me up and asked me if I could go to meet him on the weekend and said that it was urgent. I agreed to meet him.

Hari said, "I have decided to go to the U.S and have submitted my resignation even."

"Oh I see..." I brooded and asked, "What about your grand pa?"

"He will be going with us."

Everything had already been arranged. He was to take his parents with him. They had sold their ancestral property given the need of hefty cash. Hari's father was excited and happy when his son had finally agreed to his prolonged proposal of settling in the States. The American culture had never interested Hari. He always cherished and respected the society he had grown up in. He just loved being in and around Kalimpong which meant the world to him. But now he was determined to escape. It seemed better that way for so many different reasons.

Time surely heals our wounds and the pain goes
away, but deep down somewhere, somehow,
we let some kind of pain to linger on

Chapter XLIV

He Leaves

28 November 2011. He was to leave for the States. He came to my place, the evening before he left, to meet me, perhaps for the last time. He had come to me with a big bag entrusting me its responsibility.

"Especially this box, please keep it safely," He emphasized.

I, like an obedient child kept his things in safety without trying to interrupt any further. Hari spoke again, "Hey thanks for everything you have done for me. You'll always remain my best friend and I might surprise you some day."

I asked if I could accompany him till Bagdogra Airport but he denied my assistance and rather asked to pray for her, which I did and I do till date. How difficult it must be for that man who searched for love always and in return received some mixed inexplicable emotions? What thoughts might have rushed into his head that made him to leave? How many thoughts must have clashed in his wavering mind before he thought of leaving his treasured abode? What might have he felt and thought about his imperfect tales of love which engulfed him like the tide in the sea and swept his heart off love that made him deserted. How he must have felt in his life after having lost his love, not once but thrice! Many things must have had happened in his heart and mind, you and I can only imagine.

He called me after reaching Delhi and that was the last that I heard from him. Hari, whom I detested earlier and who became my dear friend later, was not there around me and I felt his absence vividly. But he must have felt a vacuum much greater, when he was left all alone in the path of love.

I hated to like him then but now I hate not to...

Part IV

One and a half year later

Chapter XLV

You Know Me

October, 2013. I was woken up by an unknown phone call. I looked at my watch it was around 12:30 am. I received the call but nobody responded from the other end. I waited for some time without any trace of a voice, though the call was on progress. I hung up cursing and tried to get back to sleep but the phone call had already made me all agog. I kept tossing and turning on my bed. It must have probably been two in the morning. I was slowly moving into the state of trance when my bed suddenly began to tremor. At first I thought an earthquake had struck once again but the movement was somewhat different and it took me a while to realize that it was definitely not what I was thinking. Well then what was it? My whole body suddenly grew heavy with this thought. I wanted to get up but something was pulling me down. I wanted to scream for help. I tried hard but I couldn't just be audible. I then tried to murmur all the chants that I knew from the Vedic texts. I realized, though I knew some by heart, I just could not recite it.

I felt something strange then. I realized that someone was there on my bed very near to me. My body grew insanely heavy but I just didn't want to lose my guts as I knew if I did, it might have an adverse effect on me. Then to cross check, I slowly moved my leg a bit towards the wall. However, I didn't take my foot out of the quilt. I sensed a part of someone else's body and got convinced that I was not alone that night, at least at that moment. I found it really eerie. I recited the chants of all that I could remember and tried to motivate myself by reminding that a guy should not be scared and that I belonged to a creed of the braves – 'the Gorkhas', and most importantly, dawn was just couple of hours due. I moved my body a bit and there I could feel a body of a man. I wanted to turn to the other side. I tried too but I just couldn't muster up my guts. I lay on my bed petrified!

I don't know how long I stayed glued. What I can only recount is that I was desperately waiting for the morning rays, soaking heavily with sweat. It was too much, I couldn't just stay like that and out of nowhere I happened to blurt out in frustration,

"Who are you?"

"You know me," Was the instant reply and whoever it was just sliced his hand on my chest and kept it there.

I couldn't muster up the courage of removing the icy hand which lay heavily on my chest. But then other things engrossed my mind. I suddenly felt fear deserting me and was more concerned in deciphering the voice I had just heard. More so the voice had said "You know me." Then it struck me – Yes I certainly knew the voice, it sounded so familiar. I had encountered it so many times in the past. The next moment I found myself in an emotional retreat with footage of yesteryears coming vividly in my memory lane. The voice reminded me of my village, my old days, my old friend, and everything started making sense to me in an abrupt way though. And when it did my eyes became moist and I could feel tears rolling down my cheeks. I don't know when I fell asleep.

*

I woke up in the morning totally perplexed. Was it a dream or was it for real. If it was a dream it was definitely an experience of a lifetime. And if it was real it was something which I would not have liked to happen. But was it some kind of a message? I still remember the happenings so vividly as if it had occurred to me yesterday. I am still flummoxed what that meant and till date it gives me a strange and bizarre feeling.

Next morning I got up; was lost in contemplation for a long time. I thought of so many things and found myself packing my belongings and headed towards home though I didn't have any concrete reasons. When I reached home I discussed the eerie happening with my parents who were vague in their answers.

I was in my room still totally perplexed. Suddenly a thought struck me and I headed towards my cupboard. I brought out the box which Hari had asked me to keep on his behalf. My curiosity made me explore its content. I didn't have the key or the consent to open it but the next moment I did unbolt it. There in that box were four diaries, knick knacks, cards and letters and a memory card. I took out the diary and started reading. I read all the letters and the diaries within the next two days. I still remember it was one in the morning when I finished reading them. I put it back in its respective place with care; opened my lap top and wrote "I have a story to tell. The man I am going to recount has nothing out of the ordinary…."

*

20 December 2014, Delhi – Fourteen months later I had finally completed the novel. Till morning I was thinking that his description would be my last words of his story. I wanted to take a day out and just relax. I was immersed in my thoughts thinking how the story would turn out to be and things alike.

I was sitting at Nehru Park which is near to the hotel I was staying. I noticed a lady and somehow she seemed very familiar. Our eyes met and we stared at each other for a while. I tried hard recalling where had I seen her! I couldn't control my curiosity any longer, so I went near her and asked, "Do we know each other?"

"I don't know but I think we have met somewhere, I just don't know where," The lady replied.

Just then a man in his early thirties came holding a baby and as he approached near he said, "Honey lets go we are getting late," and started to walk away.

"Aakash, wait!" Said the lady and turning towards me added, "Hope to see you again someday," They left the park with their baby.

As they left I happened to see the face of the child and I was taken back. It was almost a replica of Hari, a small face, long nose and a wheatish complexion with black eyes but this time very attractive. The world before me began to swirl and I lay there completely dazed and confused for some time. I cracked my head for what it could possibly be. Then I figured out it was none other than Reema. I ran towards the direction they had gone but I couldn't find them. I came back and sat on that very bench where I was sitting moments earlier. So many thoughts intrigued me.

Did his story with Reema really end at the point where I had ended? Had Hari not told me a few more things? Could there be something which he could not even write in his diary? Can it be possible for him to be unaware of so many things? Or was it just a coincidence? I don't have answers to these yet. So I leave it to you!

Some Stories are representations but all representations
are not stories until love embraces its strife

Epilogue

I guess we were destined to separate. This friend of mine never came back again, at least till now. Now all that is left of him are his memories, his imperfections which linger in my memory now and then. I actually yearn for him. How I wish I had a little bit of him. At times I need him so much to fight my own negativity in life. At times I have even tried to emulate him but without any success. He was an epitome of selflessness and optimism. Perhaps such goodness is alien to this world and even if we come across some, they stay with us only for a little while and like a sudden gush of wind in a sunny day, it goes away. I have given up my hope in him and I also know I can't be like him. Only he can play that role. May be there are few who can but I am yet to come across such a breed. But I feel him sometimes deep down within me and have lots of respect for his belief in goodness.

The moments spent with him were precious. Perhaps moments are the only thing which we can gift others; a gift which will never be old, stolen or lost; moments that would remain eternal. He used to tell me small things are the ones which are the most important ones. After all, little strokes finally make up the larger picture in the canvas. Now I understand and believe that most of his beliefs were right, indeed epigrammatic.

And I always feel that his life was round and round and round just as the hills are.